MARIE O'REGAN

THE LAST GHOST
AND
OTHER STORIES

First published by Luna Press Publishing, Edinburgh, 2019

Someone To Watch Over You. *Terror Tales of London, ed. Paul Finch, Gray Friar Press, 2013.*
The Cradle in the Corner. *Hauntings, ed. Ian Whates, Newcon Press, 2012.*
Play Time. *Darc Karnivale, ed. David Byron & Cory R. Scales, 2010.*
In The Howling of the Wind. *Estronomicon, Christmas 2008 edited by Steve Upham, 2008.*
Sleeping Black. *Great British Horror Vol. 2, Dark Satanic Mills, edited by Steve Shaw, Black Shuck Books, 2017.*
Suicide Bridge. *www.quantummuse.com, 2001.*
The Last Ghost (original to this collection)

www.lunapresspublishing.com
ISBN-13: 978-1-911143-71-0

For Paul, with love. Always.

Contents

Hearth of Darkness

There's a secret to writing supernatural stories; simplicity.

When authors over-explain or spend pages trying to make you believe their central idea, the simplicity vanishes. But ordinary people who feel they've had supernatural experiences always describe them simply, and that's their greatest power.

Simplicity is much harder than it looks.

Marie O'Regan has that power. Her tales have the timeless quality of stories told by relatives over the heads of children who are meant to be in bed. Some of these tales might have been written in the 1940s, or perhaps they were always here, waiting to be told.

Railway platforms, playgrounds, nurseries, the sound of the wind, a handprint on a wall, a room in shadow, a house too quiet. Marie catches the quiet human moments too many of the more baroque, psychological writers have forgotten. Her ghosts are in the home, where all stories start.

So think of these as tales your mother secretly knew about but felt uncomfortable telling you. She doesn't have to do it now. Marie is here to do it for you.

Christopher Fowler
August, 2018

Foreword

It's no secret that I love ghost stories—I've written quite a few myself, I also edited *The Mammoth Book of Ghost Stories by Women* and *Phantoms...* there is nothing quite like reading a ghost story, preferably when it's cold outside, and the lights are on, the curtains drawn. They evoke an atmosphere that's quite unlike any other type of tale, a feeling of sadness and longing, and at times even sympathy for the poor deceased creature so desperate to impart their story to the living.

What I haven't done, so far, is collect any of my own ghost stories into one specifically themed volume, so I'm very grateful to Francesca and Rob of Luna Press for giving me the chance to do just that. Here you'll find "The Last Ghost", a young girl's tale of loss; "In The Howling of the Wind", a small boy waiting for his parents in a house suddenly grown strange; "Someone To Watch Over You", the story of a protective phantom; "The Cradle in the Corner", a slightly different haunting; "Play Time", a cautionary tale on the dangers of playing out alone at night; "Sleeping Black", a tale of vengeful spirits awoken by a house's new tenants, and "Suicide Bridge", a love story with a difference.

One thing I hadn't realised, until now, was quite how many of my ghost stories involve children, in one way or another—perhaps it's because children see more, and judge less; perhaps it's that they're more empathetic than the rest of us, or easier for us to empathise with. Who knows? Either way, you'll find within these pages some of my favourite stories from those I've written; I hope you find something that becomes a favourite of yours.

Marie O'Regan
Derbyshire, July 2018

Someone To Watch Over You

Emily glanced over her shoulder again, hoping to find nothing—but her shadow was still there, keeping pace. She sped up, annoyed to find that the increased tempo of the tap-tap of her heels was making her feel worse, not better—the fact that they'd picked up a gruffer echo was something she tried to ignore. She was only a few feet from the stairs leading down to the exit now; and she cursed her penchant for sitting at the front of the train—all it had done was leave her with further to go to get to safety.

The lights in the waiting room went out, and she moaned—thank God she was at the stairs now. What on earth had possessed her to wait till the last train home when she knew damn well how dark it got on the platform at this time of night? East Finchley was a beautiful Art Deco station, but it was also the first station going northwards that wasn't underground—and when the staff switched the waiting room lights off, it got dark quickly.

She heard her pursuer's breathing quicken and grow ragged as he started to run, and she launched herself at the stairs with little thought of how hard it would be to keep her balance at that speed. She clattered downwards, praying someone would hear her and come to investigate—but no one did. Towards the bottom she tripped, and felt herself grasped by strong arms—her rescuer stood her up and moved on before she had a chance to register who it was; her only impression was of strength and the cloying smell of tobacco smoke.

Then he was gone. She stood in the corridor and stared upward, scared her pursuer would still follow—there was a scuffle up there, then a cry, and finally the sound of squealing brakes as the last southbound train was brought to a sudden halt. An alarm sounded and she blanched, knowing what had happened. She just didn't know to whom. A shadow moved at the top of the stairs, and she saw a man's silhouette against the lights of the incoming train—a tall figure in a long, dark coat; a hat obscuring his features. He seemed to look down at her, just for a moment, and then he was gone.

Now staff arrived. She found herself shouldered to one side as guards ran up the stairs, and a very nervous young man tapped her arm, tried to shepherd her back towards the ticket offices, and the way out. "If you'd come this way, Miss…"

She nodded, and allowed herself to be led. From behind her came the unmistakeable sound of someone throwing up.

*

As she walked into the office next morning, chatter stilled—she saw heads turn as she passed by, eyes drop as she sought to engage them and find out what was so interesting. Then she saw her boss, George Burrows, appear at his door and beckon her into his office, and her heart sank.

"If I could have a word, Miss Lane," he said, and stood back to allow her entrance.

She nodded and swept past him, trying to ignore the nervous muttering that swelled behind her.

He followed her in and indicated the chair opposite his, and waited till they were both seated before he continued. "I'm surprised to see you in this morning," he said, his tone kind.

"You are?"

"You've been up most of the night, after all," he went on. He registered the incomprehension on her face and smiled. "This is a newspaper, Emily, surely you realised we'd hear of a death on the line?"

Realisation dawned, and Emily was embarrassed. "I didn't think. I mean, I knew you'd hear about the body on the line, I just didn't connect the fact you'd find out I was on scene, as it were."

"You're tired, of course," George said. "There's no reason for you to be up to speed with the office at this hour." He pressed a button on his intercom and spoke to his secretary. "Can you bring those files in, please, Carole?"

The door opened almost immediately, and Carole swept in

with a manila folder clutched to her frail chest, tattered pieces of paper creeping from its edges. She smiled at Emily, before a "humph" from George dissolved her grin and sent her scuttling back to her desk.

George opened the file, and took out various clippings—placing them side by side on the desk before her. "You're not the first one, you see."

"I'm not the first one…? I'm not following you."

He tapped the clippings, impatient now. "Look! It's right there, see?" He sighed at her confused expression, and sat back. "I wouldn't be a million miles from the truth if I said you were about to be attacked before this happened, am I right?"

Emily stared. "How…?"

"Look at the clippings," he said. "There have been a number of instances of 'phantom rescues' over the years; yours is just the latest."

"Phantom what?" Emily laughed. "I'm sorry, but just because I got the willies late at night on a train platform doesn't mean I was attacked."

"What were you scared of? Last night, on the platform?"

Emily laughed. "It sounds stupid now, but I thought someone was following me."

"And you felt threatened, yes?" George was bending forward now, his hands clasped in front of him, a finger on his lips.

Emily nodded. "Of course. A woman on her own, late at night, no one around… and someone's walking behind you, at the same pace as you, speeding up when you do…" She stopped, spooked all over again, her mind back with the events of the previous night, the man's heavy footsteps catching up with her own, each heel tap accompanied by a deeper echo …

"Of course." George sat back, satisfied he was right. "And then someone appeared, out of the night, and saved you."

"He saved me from falling, I suppose," she conceded, "but I hadn't actually been attacked, had I. I just got scared."

George shook his head. "I believe you were about to be attacked, and if you're honest," here he stared at her over his half-rim glasses, his expression serious, "so do you."

Emily attempted a smile, but failed miserably. "Because it's happened before, right?"

"That's right," he said, nodding. "Read the clippings."

The clippings were of varying age, she saw, from issues of the paper as far back as the 1970s. All told similar tales—a young girl leaving the station late at night, complaining of a sense of being followed—a man attempting to catch up with them. All the girls had been grabbed at the head of the stairs (she'd been lucky, she realised, to get down them without being caught) and pulled towards the darkened waiting room. So far, so unsurprising. The odd fact was that, in each case, the girl concerned spoke of the smell of pipe smoke, and strong arms wrestling them away from their attackers… and a brief glimpse of a manly shape in a long dark overcoat with square shoulders and a hat, brim down over the eyes, as it descended upon their assailant; a style that had been old-fashioned enough to stand out, even then.

Stapled behind each of these clippings was a shorter article from the following day—a tale of a body on the tracks, no sign of a struggle. One girl had seen her rescuer fall onto the line alongside her attacker, and screamed until help came—but the railway workers thus summoned only found the body of her attacker; there was no trace of anyone else having been at the scene.

She placed the clippings back in the folder, congratulating herself on the fact that the shaking in her fingers was almost imperceptible, and let out a breath. "They can't all be the same."

"And yet the similarities just keep stacking up."

"Someone's exaggerating, making things up."

George sat forward, frowning. "That doesn't track though, Emily, does it. Different people, different times… yet all tell of a man in a coat and hat."

"Doesn't have to be the same man," Emily pointed out.

"I'll grant you that in the forties a lot of men wore dark coats and hats," he said. "But what about since then? And all of them smelled of pipe tobacco?"

"Lots of people smoke," she tried… but she could see George already shaking his head.

"Not pipes," he said, sighing. "It's a very different smell, as you know. And besides, not that many people smoke anymore, compared to then. I mean, look at films—in the seventies everyone was doing it. Not these days, though; these days if a character in a movie smokes, he's usually a baddie."

Emily had no answers. "I didn't really see anyone," she said. "Just felt his arms, and smelled the tobacco."

"So you do admit it was tobacco and not a fag you smelled?"

"I have to, don't I," she said. "It was Dad's brand, Old Holborn."

"And the man was wearing a long coat, and a hat, just like the other times?"

Emily nodded. "I don't know what kind of hat, though… the name, I mean. It was like those old films—with that actor Dad loved. James Mason."

George laughed. "God, that's right—he did, didn't he?"

Emily stared out at her colleagues; all staring in, amazed he was laughing. "George, they're looking."

He frowned again, but the corners of his mouth were twitching, and Emily knew he'd be laughing again before long. He and Dad had been two of a kind that way, and she felt his loss all the more keenly when she was with her uncle.

"All right, lass," he said. "Best get out there and investigate this, eh? We wouldn't want everyone knowing the cub reporter's my favourite niece."

She smiled, then scraped her chair back and stood up. Leaning forward to pick up the files she whispered, "Can I come and see you and Auntie Ann on Sunday?"

"'Course you can," he said. "Can't see you doing a roast, somehow."

She grinned and held the files tight as she turned, forcing herself to look serious. "See you then, then."

*

Two hours later, poring over the files she'd found in the paper's archives, Emily was forced to admit George had been right. East

Finchley station had, over the years, been prey to a number of these incidents—the earliest one she'd found had happened in October of 1972 when a seventeen-year-old girl had been coming home from a day visiting family in Camden Town. She'd been followed as she got off the train, and grabbed before she reached the stairs leading down to the exit. The only witness had been a middle-aged man in a black overcoat and a grey hat, who'd shouted for help and run to her aid. The two men had scuffled, and in the melée the girl had been thrown to the floor. She'd struggled to her knees just in time to see the older man grab her attacker as he made for her once more, knife in hand. In the struggle, both men had apparently overbalanced and fallen on to the tracks, into the path of an oncoming train. Both had died almost instantly.

No one had listened to the victim's protestations that her saviour hadn't fallen; he'd *pulled* her attacker down onto the tracks, and held him there as the train bore down on both of them. Emily didn't believe it either; who would willingly go to their own death, when all they'd had to do, really, was knock the attacker down and pin him there until help arrived—which in a staffed underground station shouldn't have taken more than a minute or two?

She spent another hour going through various other reports from over the years, but none seemed to quite fit the facts of what she'd been told by her uncle. There was a long and dispiriting list of the usual muggings, fights and accidents—some resulting in death, others in injury—none of these mentioned the man in the hat and overcoat.

Looking at the clock, Emily was surprised to see it was almost four o'clock; she hadn't even taken a lunch break, or had a coffee. No wonder she felt sick.

A shadow appeared at her left side and, looking up, she saw her uncle there, frowning again. "Any progress?"

She shook her head. "Not much; the usual list of violence—brawls, attacks, not much else." She reached into the hanging drawer on her right and drew out her handbag. "Do you mind if I go home a bit early? I've got a thumping headache."

"I'm not surprised," he answered. "You haven't left your desk all day, and you can't have got much sleep last night." He started to walk back to his office. "Go home, get some rest, but clear your desk first."

She nodded. "I will. Thank you."

"Bright and early tomorrow, mind," he called. "And I'll expect some progress tomorrow, alright?"

She groaned. She knew she'd better have something he could run by the end of the next day, but had no idea what to write. She trudged towards the exit, shoulders bowed. She'd worry about that later.

*

Twenty minutes later she was sitting on a train, heading back towards East Finchley. She glanced at her watch, and was comforted to find it was only four thirty. There should be plenty of people about when she reached her destination.

Sure enough, she hit the beginning of the rush hour, and East Finchley was teeming with people as she got off the tube and headed for the stairs. She couldn't help being over-cautious, jumping when anyone got too close—which earned her more than a few dodgy looks from people who couldn't decide if she was on drugs, drunk or just plain crazy. She was starting to think they might have a point—perhaps she was mad, after all. As she turned left at the bottom of the stairs, heading towards the ticket barrier and the High Road, she caught a glimpse of a hat. A very old-fashioned hat that looked uncomfortably familiar. The crowds parted and she saw that the hat belonged to an elderly gentleman, being buffeted towards her by the evening tide of commuters.

She stood back to let him pass, earning herself a few choice comments in the process, but she didn't care—he looked worried enough without being accosted by a loon of a woman demanding to know where he'd got his hat.

Keeping her head down so she didn't find herself getting into even more trouble, she made her way out to the High Road and hopped on a bus heading towards North Finchley. Twenty minutes later, she was letting herself into her flat above a shop just off Tally Ho Corner, trying not to fall over the cat winding its way between her feet and purring. "Come on, puss," she said, nudging the animal gently with her toe. The cat jumped and started off towards the kitchen. Emily laughed, shedding her jacket onto the bannisters as she followed. "You've got me right where you want me, don't you?"

Later, dinner cooked and eaten, cat fed and watered, Emily found herself channel-hopping as she thought over the events of the previous twenty-four hours. She felt such a fraud—it wasn't as if the man at the station the previous night had actually attacked her, after all. She'd been scared, yes, and he might well have tried to drag her off if the man in the hat hadn't…

Hadn't what, exactly?

She'd felt someone. She had. The feel of his body as he pulled her upright and the smell of pipe smoke that rose from his damp wool coat; she couldn't have imagined that. She examined her arms, and was a little surprised to find no trace of his clasp. He'd *hauled* her to her feet; surely there should be a mark? Something to show the strength of his grip? Whoever had been following her had definitely felt his strength—her rescuer had swept him off the platform to his death. Hadn't he?

She tried to focus on the TV screen before her, aware she'd just missed something important. Offering up a silent prayer of thanks to the great god Sky Plus, she picked up the remote and rewound. The local news was on, and a reporter was standing outside East Finchley station, microphone in hand, with a suitably solemn expression on his face. He was reporting the apparent suicide of a young man the previous night—a Warren Lytton, nineteen years old, a history of minor problems with the police; a couple of mugging convictions that seemed to consist more of aggravated shoving than outright violence, no one had been hurt; shoplifting… nothing too sinister.

Someone just off-camera was shouting, and Emily strained to hear what was being said. No use; whoever it was had been pushed out of range of the microphone, and all she could make out was raised voices. A female voice, shouting, and more voices speaking in a conciliatory tone. The reporter stopped speaking, and in the silence that followed Emily heard quite clearly: "My boy wouldn't kill himself! He wouldn't do that!" The report cut back to the studio, and the newscaster shaking his head in disapproval.

Emily turned the TV off, her stomach churning. She ran for the bathroom and just made it in time before she doubled over and lost her supper. She sank to the floor, shaking, and wiped the sweat from her face. So it was being labelled a suicide. Perhaps it even had been, who was she to say? She couldn't help feeling a sense of relief that it was over—she'd been dreading more questions by the police. They'd been lovely to her, calming her down and taking her home—but no one had taken her story of the man in the hat seriously, that was obvious. She supposed in the absence of any sign of someone else at the scene they'd had no choice—no one else had even seen him.

She found herself crying, and rubbed her face clean of tears. She would not let this get to her. It was done, and she could move on now. She'd file a piece in the morning about the suicide, and that would be the end of it.

She smelled pipe smoke, and flashed back to the tunnel—she had seen him, she knew. So why had no one else?

*

The next morning found her at her desk bright and early, typing up the report of Warren Lytton's apparent suicide—she felt someone standing beside her and looked up to see George, reading the copy as she typed it.

"What about the attack?" he asked.

Emily shrugged. "What can I say? There's no record of anyone else being seen at the station at that time, just this guy. Who knows? Maybe he slipped off the platform running away."

"You don't believe that."

"No," she answered. "I don't. But I don't want to look like an idiot, or crazy."

He said nothing.

"Would you?" she pushed.

George stared at her for a long moment before nodding. "Fair enough." Then he was gone.

Emily sat, nonplussed, not entirely sure from their exchange whether she should go ahead and file the piece or not. Gradually the office started to fill up, chatter replacing the peace of a few moments before; not making things any easier to focus on. Someone laughed and she whirled round, the voice familiar, but no one seemed to be responsible—most of her colleagues were by now seated at their desks, concentrating on the monitors in front of them.

She tried to work out why the laugh was familiar, but to no avail—it had been a man's voice, of that she was sure; probably an older man, but no one in her immediate area fitted that description.

Her nostrils filled with the scent of Old Holborn and tears welled up as she thought of her father; she'd loved to sit on his lap as a child, and this smell brought her back to those days in an instant. Yet no one around her was smoking.

She gave up, and sent her article to her editor, then closed the screen down. She needed some air.

As she left the building, someone jostled her, and as she automatically apologised she realised this was no accident. Her attacker's mother stood before her, her expression furious. Emily glanced back over her shoulder to see if anyone was on hand to help should it be necessary, but she was on her own.

"Excuse me," she said, and moved to side-step the woman.

Mrs Lytton, however, was having none of this. She stepped in front of Emily once more, her eyes narrowed.

Emily wondered if she thought this made her appear more intimidating, and bit down on the smile that threatened to bloom. Perhaps she'd have found it more frightening if she hadn't found herself looking down at the older woman.

Mrs Lytton took a step forward, not content till she was close enough to share Emily's breath, something Emily found vaguely distasteful, but not particularly scary.

"My boy didn't kill himself," she spat.

Emily nodded. "You might be right," she said before adding with uncharacteristic cruelty: "But he's dead, so we can't ask him, can we?"

The woman gasped, and now she didn't look threatening—she looked heartbroken, and Emily felt heat blossom in her chest before spreading to her face. How could she have said that?

"I'm sorry," she said. "I didn't mean it to sound so…"

"Fucking cruel?" Mrs Lytton interrupted, and Emily had the grace to look sorry.

She nodded. "I'm sorry he's dead, I really am. But it's not my fault."

"Then whose is it?" the woman wailed. "Who killed my boy?"

Emma sighed, and steeled herself for the inevitable response to what came next. "I didn't see anyone," she said. "I just heard a cry, and then the alarm. I was running away."

"From what?"

"From Warren." The woman hissed as if scalded, and Emma hurried to apologise. "I'm really sorry, but he was chasing me… and then he was gone, and I heard him yell… and then there were brakes, and…"

"Stop it!" Mrs Lytton screamed, raising her arms as if to fend Emily off. "Bloody stop it, you lying bitch!" Her hand was up and planted firmly against Emily's cheek before either of them knew it was going to happen, and then she was gone, leaving Emily alone and sobbing, hand raised to the livid imprint on her shocked face.

Emily caught a whiff of that tobacco again, and shook her head. "No," she said. "Please don't." The smell faded, and she breathed out a juddering sigh of relief, "I'm going home," she said, to no one. "Alone."

No one followed.

*

Emily's piece came out the following day, and her phone started to ring as people realised she'd been involved.

The article made no mention of the attack she'd been sure was about to follow, but did mention her presence at the station; she found herself to be a celebrity, and decided—with her uncle's permission—to stay indoors for a few days, until something else of interest happened and she was no longer 'interesting' to the gawkers and on-lookers that had crawled out of the woodwork.

*

A few days later Emily found herself making her way home alone once more, having spent the evening at a local theatre for a review of a play being put on by the local amateur dramatics society. *Blithe Spirit.* The joke wasn't lost, but Emily didn't think she'd ever find that funny again.

As she left East Finchley station, she saw a man leaning against the wall, hat pulled down low over his face, shoulders hunched against the cold. She slowed, then drew herself up and hurried forward—she'd be safe inside.

The man stood up as she approached, and as he lifted his head she saw she'd been scared of nothing.

"Uncle George," she said. "I wasn't expecting to see you here."

He smiled. "I thought you might want some company. Seeing as it's late."

"I'm glad you came. It's a bit quiet tonight, isn't it?"

George nodded, and took her arm. "Come on, we'll take the bus."

Emily found herself propelled down the hill, towards the bridge. "I normally get the bus at the next stop up," she said, trying to pull away. "It's a bit dark this way."

The bus stop they were heading to was closer, she knew, but she didn't like going under the bridge where it was dark. And there was a stretch of road just beyond the adjacent pub that was bordered by gardens with overhanging bushes—she preferred to be more visible, especially after...

George sighed, impatient. "It's all right, I'm with you." And kept pulling her on, past the bus stop they should have waited at.

As they reached the corner of Bishops Avenue, George pushed her to the side, and she found herself by a house with a low fence—and a lot of foliage.

"What are you doing?"

George laughed. "I thought we could take a bit of a walk."

"Why down here?"

George's grip on her arm grew painful, and she got ready to scream.

"Uncle George, what's going on? You're scaring me!"

"I'm sorry, love," he said. "I didn't want to do that. I just wanted you to see. I want you to make everyone see."

"You're not making any sense," she said. "See what?"

George nodded at the house, but had the grace to loosen his grip. "He lived here."

"Who did?"

"Your saviour. You were right; he's done this before—and it's time people knew."

Emily turned to stare at the house—unprepossessing in the gloom, she could see, nevertheless, that it was neglected. An air of loneliness pervaded its surrounds, making it stand out from the expensive, well-tended houses that adjoined it. "Who lived here?" she asked.

"A man called Arthur Fuller. I went to school with him, or rather your dad did. They were a couple of years below me."

"He knew Dad?"

"Very well. They were mates."

"What happened to him?"

George's eyes glittered as he started to talk. "He was killed. Walking home one night, late, he saw a girl being attacked by some thug at East Finchley station. Decided he had to have a go, save the girl." He laughed, the sound bitter in his throat. "Bloody idiot."

Emily didn't quite understand. "Why was he an idiot, if all he did was try to help someone?"

"The girl was your mother, and Arthur knew her, of course."

Emily stared.

"You look like her, you know," he said; and tried to touch her hair.

She flinched.

George grinned, his teeth bared white in the dark. "You see? You're just like her."

She took a step back, and he gripped her arm tighter.

"It's not like she was going out with your dad at the time," he said. "She was fair game."

"Oh, George," Emily moaned. "You were the thug?"

"So the papers called me. I just wanted a kiss, that's all. But she wouldn't be quiet."

"And Arthur heard her? Came to help?"

George nodded. "I always felt bad that he got hurt. I just pushed him off. I didn't see the car coming."

The smell of Old Holborn surrounded her now, and she felt herself relax. They weren't on their own any more.

George took a step towards her, and Emily stiffened. "I want you to tell his story," he said. "I want people to know he's still saving people."

"Why?" she asked. "Because you feel guilty?"

George nodded. "That, yes, and because people should know it wasn't just an accident. He was a good bloke, and he tried to help your mum. Just like he's still trying to help people."

Emily took George's hand, and peeled his fingers away from her arm, one by one. "I can't do that," she said. "It wouldn't be right."

"Why not?" he demanded. "Why shouldn't he get some recognition for what he did?"

"Because then they'd know what you did," she said, and saw the realisation dawn in his eyes. "And, even worse, what you nearly did to Mum."

George launched himself forward and pushed her towards the busy road.

She felt herself falling, but was overwhelmed by the scent of pipe tobacco, even as she felt herself being set back on her feet. She stood, gasping, as she saw the cloud darken around her uncle, a smoky figure reaching out for him and drawing him towards the main road. A bus was hurtling up the hill towards them, but she couldn't make a sound—and it was too dark for them to be seen, just yet.

George was trying hard to break free, but to no avail. As the bus drew close, the cloud solidified, and Emily saw her saviour, hat pulled low over his face, dark coat pulled tight around him. He pushed George down, and both men fell under the oncoming vehicle—brakes squealed, someone screamed, and Emily found herself witnessing everything this time, at close range, as Arthur held him there.

She saw George's hand, protruding from underneath the front of the bus—blood trickling towards the kerb. There was no sign of the rest of him. The hand twitched, just once, then was still. A woman who'd been walking up the main road was screaming: scream after scream pealing out, with barely time to breathe between. The bus driver was sitting in his cab, head buried in his hands—the few passengers were staring forward, shock etched on their faces. She could already hear the sirens.

Emily staggered to the kerb and threw up, and when she looked up, he was there. He smiled at her, and touched his fingers to his hat—an old-world gesture. The smell of Old Holborn caused her stomach to clench, and she vomited again. When she looked up again, he was gone.

She couldn't tell the story, she realised. And not because it would ruin her aunt's life, and her parents' memory. She couldn't tell the story because then everyone would know about Arthur— and much as she hated the idea of him continuing his vendetta, she hated even more the idea that he wouldn't be able to help any more girls daft enough to wander home on their own in dangerous places.

The Cradle in the Corner

Mary stared in horror at the monstrosity standing before her.

"Do you like it?" Alan asked. He stood there, all proud of himself—chest puffed out, huge grin on his face. How was she supposed to destroy that?

She released a breath that shook on its way out into the world, surprised not to see actual smoke. *Calm, woman. He thinks he's done a good thing.* "It's… different, I'll say that for it."

The smile froze, and she rushed to smooth things over, make it better, as usual. He was only trying to do something nice. "I haven't seen one like that before. Where'd you get it?"

The smile returned and Adam knelt by the cot, eager for his wife to share his enthusiasm. "In a little antique store in town; I know how much you love old things."

She laughed. "It's definitely got that going for it."

Alan sat back, his face serious now. "I know this needs work, love, but that's what I want—a project. And once it's been painted, got the right drapes and stuff—you'll see; it'll be beautiful." He leaned across and passed her a leaflet he'd picked up from the carpet. "See? That's what it should look like when it's done."

The cot in the picture was far from today's image of a wooden cot with bars up the sides and a high mattress. This one looked more like a laundry basket on legs; wire frame on crossed iron legs that resembled the bottom of a laundry rack—a precursor to today's Moses basket, sort of. A cradle, rather than a cot, and in lamentable condition. Mary smiled, feeling slightly better—a cradle was only for a little while. "It's beautiful, love. Will it be safe, though?"

He nodded. "Yep; by the time the baby's big enough to sit up, she'll have moved on to a cot. The cradle can be stored away at that point." He looked up, then, eyes sparkling as he asked, "Where do you want it?"

Looking round the bedroom, with its low eaves and quirky

corners, Mary was at a loss for a moment. Then she saw the perfect spot. There was a recess by the window on the east side of the room that featured a cushioned window seat that she could sit on while she fed the baby, or sang her to sleep. The window itself was double glazed, secure from draughts, and caught the sunrise every morning. "Over there," she said. "In the corner, by the window."

Alan grinned, and hefted the cradle over to the indicated spot, angling it so that it wasn't too close to the window itself, yet would catch the sun's warmth during the day. "Perfect," he said. "Looks like it's always been there."

Mary shivered as a shadow passed in front of her, obscuring the sun and letting a sudden chill into the room. The cradle looked wrong, now—cold and hard—bare as it was of any drapes or covers. The metal seemed to darken before her eyes, and there was an odour of mildew, and decay. "Put it away for now, love," she said, and moved away. "Let's go downstairs and have a cuppa."

Alan looked up, then, and frowned when he saw his wife. "You okay? You look really pale."

She crossed her hands over her bump, protective of her child even as it kicked playfully against her palm, and backed towards the door. "I'm fine, just a headache…" then she was gone, her footsteps thudding down the stairs as she headed for the kitchen.

*

"Feeling better?"

Alan's voice broke Mary's concentration, and she blinked as she registered his presence. She was sitting in the rocking chair by the fireplace, rocking blankly back and forth as she stared into the dormant hearth—her concentration had been absolute, but she couldn't for the life of her remember what she'd been thinking about. She nodded, and took the cup of tea he offered gratefully, cupping it in her hands, eager for warmth.

"I am, thanks," she said. "I can't think what came over me."

"You're bound to get queasy or achy now and again, I suppose," he answered. "You've still got what, six weeks to go?"

"About that," she agreed. "Maybe I just need something to eat."

He grinned as he put a plate of toast beside her. "Thought you might say that."

"You know me too well," she said, "thanks, love." She took a piece of toast and grinned as she sat back. "This baby's going to be the size of a whale, I'm sure. All I do is eat."

"It's nice to see," he answered. "At least you're not being sick all the time now."

"True."

Mary cocked her head as something creaked overhead. "You know, we really ought to get those floorboards checked." The noise came again, louder this time, as something moved across the bedroom floor.

Alan sat quiet, listening. "Either something's wrong with the floorboards or the cat's so heavy she sounds like a person, now."

Mary choked on her toast, laughing. The laughter died when she saw Rags lying on the rug in front of the fire, looking like nothing more than a huge, furry cushion. "Definitely not Rags."

There came the sound of a door closing, and then the house was quiet. Both Mary and Alan sat watching the cat, listening to the usual sounds—the clock on the mantel ticking, the boiler clicking on as the temperature dropped, water rushing in the pipes—but no more creaking overhead. For a moment Mary wondered if it might be sounds from next door, but then she remembered this cottage was detached. It had been their dream home, and they'd only bought it when they started trying for a baby.

"This is an old house," Alan offered. "Bound to make noises; it'll be the floorboards settling, or something like that."

Mary nodded. "Must be." She smiled, and turned to the toast again, her voice a little too bright as she continued, "Must be boards relaxing in the heat or something."

*

Mary lay in bed that night, twisting and turning as she tried unsuccessfully to sink into a deep and blissful sleep. Alan lay next to her, snoring gently, oblivious to her restlessness. The cherry blossom tree in the garden cast shadows that walked across the walls and ceiling, spindly branches reaching for the door on the far side of the room. The wind moaned as it sought entrance to the house, failing miserably thanks to the new windows they'd put in just before finding out Mary was pregnant. A door banged and Mary flinched, jerked into full consciousness. There was no further sound, and gradually she relaxed, happy to believe Rags was on the prowl, probably after some small creature that had braved the cat flap and gained entrance to the kitchen. She heard a faint yowl, and smiled. There was nothing Rags loved more than to present them with whatever she'd chased during the night as a gift over breakfast. Hopefully this time she'd offer it to Alan, before Mary got downstairs.

Something creaked, closer this time, and Mary froze. The creaking came again, and something moved fitfully in the darkness. Mary gazed around the room, and saw the cradle move. Shocked, she watched as it rocked, ever so slightly, in the shadows. A faint creak came again each time it moved, and Mary got out of bed, making for the window, normally draught-free; perhaps Alan hadn't shut it properly?

She reached the window and rattled the handle; nothing. The lock was securely fastened, and there was no trace of movement in the net curtains that hung there. Looking down, Mary could see the cherry trees branches whipping back and forth in the wind, but she could feel nothing of the night's fury standing by the glass.

She tested the cradle, then. It creaked once more as she rattled the frame, the noise instantly recognisable. Perhaps a screw was loose somewhere? She resolved to get Alan to check everything carefully whilst he was absorbed in his restoration project—it had to be safe before the baby came.

A wave of dizziness swept over her, making her sway. Her left hand moved automatically to protect the baby; her right finding its way to her back, which was starting to complain at this nocturnal wandering. She crept back into bed, chilled, and curled up against Alan's back, resting her icy feet against the warmth of his legs. True to form, he just pulled the duvet further up, making sure she was covered even in his sleep, and she smiled as his arm came up and rested on her hip, patting it. The baby kicked again, this time connecting with his back, and he huffed half-heartedly before settling back down. Sleep hurtled towards her, and she realised as she fell helplessly into its grip that somewhere a baby was crying.

*

The next few days were filled with the sound of Alan's off-key humming as he first sanded, then painted the cradle a beautiful shade of very pale pink, and—at her insistence—carefully checked all the screws and fastenings he could see. Humming was a habit of his when happy, and Mary liked to hear it. He insisted the cradle was safe, nothing was loose now (if anything ever had been), but she still heard creaking in the night and pictured the cradle rocking—even though she couldn't actually see it doing so. And sometimes there was a whining noise (it must be the cradle, she reasoned, it couldn't be anything else), making a sound eerily reminiscent of a fussing infant. "It must be the wind," he said, and she could hear the patience leeching out of his voice a little more every time he had to say it. Finally she gave in, and didn't mention the creaking any more—but night after night, there it was, taunting her. She couldn't sleep, and when she did manage to doze, her dreams were filled with the sound of a baby crying, and someone—a woman—wailing in the night.

Tuesday morning, and Mary woke to find Alan already dressed, ready to put a third and final coat of paint on the cradle. Fabric swatches were laid out on the dressing table for her to look at, and the window was open, letting in a chill wind.

"Morning, sleepy," he said, smiling at her. His smile faded as he looked at her, and she spoke more sharply than she'd intended.

"What?"

"Nothing," he said. "At least…"

"What, Alan?" She sat up and rubbed her eyes, shivering as the draught reached her sweat-soaked skin.

"Another bad night?"

She groaned. "Is there any other kind, these days?" Heaving

herself upright to rest her back against the pillows, she blinked and focussed on her husband's worried face. "Do I look that bad?"

"You don't look good, love, I have to say. You're feeling okay, aren't you? Apart from the sleep thing, I mean."

Mary nodded. "I'm just tired, that's all. I keep hearing that thing creaking at night—"

"It's not the—"

"I know you say it's not the cradle, but what the hell is it, otherwise?" She'd snapped before she could stop herself, and stopped before she could say something else, something hurtful.

Alan's face fell as he replied. "I don't know. I've checked the cradle, the floorboards… nothing seems to creak. Maybe you're just dreaming it?"

"Maybe I am," she said, and sighed. "I know I'm dreaming a baby crying, but either way the result's the same. I'm shattered!"

"You stay there," Alan answered. "I'll bring you breakfast in bed."

Mary saw the cradle behind her husband, and told herself it wasn't a rocking motion spied from the corner of her eye that had attracted her attention. The cradle was still now, no sign of having moved. But she could have sworn… She smiled brightly at Alan, to show him just how okay she was, and threw the covers back. "No, I'll come down. I'd rather eat at the table, with you."

Bemused, Alan could only watch as she hurried past him and into the bathroom. The door clicked shut and he heard the lock turn. And his wife started to cry. Standing by the bathroom door, he leant against the wood, put his hand to the door and listened as she tried to stifle her sobs. Silently, he willed his wife to let him in, to talk about what was causing all this. Nothing, just the sound of Mary's hitching sobs as she tried to get herself under control. Sighing, he gave up and went down to the kitchen to make them some breakfast. He could at least make sure she ate properly.

When Mary ventured into the kitchen her face glowed pink, scrubbed clean to hide her tears. She couldn't hide her eyes, though; their watery stare showed him just how upset she was, and he tried once more to solve this.

"You've been crying," he said.

Mary shook her head. "Not really. Bit weepy this morning, that's all."

"Why, love?"

"Just tired." She peered at him over her cup, her expression vague. "Probably hormones."

Ordinarily, the mention of hormones would be enough for him to leave the subject well alone. It wasn't unusual for her to get weepy at times, and pregnancy had certainly played its part in that. On the other hand…

"Are you sure that's all it is?"

Now she concentrated on the table cloth, tracing its pattern with a slightly shaky hand. She noticed its weakness and placed her hands on her lap, where the fingers proceeded to work at each other, intertwining and unlocking ceaselessly. "What else could it be?" she asked.

"The cradle, maybe?"

She flinched, and shook her head. "Don't be silly."

"I've seen the way you look at the cradle, love," he said gently. "I know you don't like it. I guess I hoped that would change when I'd finished."

She sighed. "It's not the cradle, as such," she said. "But I hear the thing creaking, night after night, and I know you say it's not the cradle but sometimes—"

"Sometimes what?"

"Sometimes I see the cradle rocking."

Alan stared at her, shocked. "That's impossible."

"I know," she wailed, "but it does!" She was crying hard now, and he didn't know what to do. She hiccupped as she went on, "and… and… and that baby keeps crying! It's driving me nuts, Alan!"

"That's… crazy, love," he whispered.

"I know it is. I know how it sounds." She wiped her eyes and took a deep, shuddering breath. "And yet it's true." She attempted a smile, then, and her next words broke Alan's heart. "Maybe I am crazy."

"No, love," he said, and went to her. He leant down and

wrapped his arms around her shoulders, held her tight. "You were right the first time, I think. Hormones. You're just worried about the baby, and it's coming out in dreams."

She snuffled against his chest. "You think so?"

"Of course," he said, willing himself to believe it. "We'll ask the doc tomorrow, when we go for your check up, okay? I'm sure everything's fine."

Mary pulled herself out of his grasp, and smiled up at him. "Hope so." She sniffed, and then grinned. "Can I smell bacon?"

Alan laughed. "You and your stomach. I cooked a full English; hang on." He busied himself with the business of sorting out the meal, and tried to look happy. Mary needed him to be strong. He could do that, if it meant she relaxed. Her face lit up as he brought her meal across, and he sat back and watched her eat, aware that this woman was his world. And he wouldn't, couldn't, let anything happen to her.

*

Night-time once more. Mary tossed and turned, and Alan watched—intent, this time, on making sure she wasn't disturbed. The cradle was silent, unmoving, and he'd pulled the curtains tight shut against any possible draught. The house sat inert—joining him in his vigil.

Midnight. The floor creaked, and Alan turned towards the noise's source—a narrow wedge of light gleamed under the door. Was someone in the hall? Noiselessly, he rose and crept towards the light, freezing as it was cut by two black bands. Someone was standing on the other side; he could hear the rasp of their breath in the dark. The bands shifted to the left, paused, and then moved back. Alan shivered, aware the temperature had plummeted—his stomach fluttering frantically as he fought to regain control of his will. His body locked itself in position just beside the door, and refused to let him try to turn the door handle. The floor creaked once more, and Alan saw the handle turn slightly. He couldn't move. Mary moaned and stirred—and the light went out, leaving everything in shadow. For long seconds he watched, and waited, but whatever had been there had been banished by his wife's movements. They were safe once more. Distantly, he heard a baby whimper, and a woman's voice shushed the child as even that distant noise faded away.

Then silence.

"Alan?"

He cried out at the sound of Mary's voice, and slumped against the door as he tried to catch his breath. "Jesus, you frightened the life out of me!"

"What is it? What's wrong?"

There was panic in her voice, and Alan switched the light on, trying to smile but terrified that his expression must be nearer to a grimace. Mary was staring, owl-eyed, at him; her face so pale. "It's all right, love. I'm sorry." He crossed over to her, sat on the edge of the bed. "I thought I heard something, that's all."

"And did you?"

"No," he lied. "Well, maybe the cat. I guess Rags needs to go on a diet after all."

She didn't smile, and he knew he wasn't fooling her for a moment. He got up and turned his bedside lamp on, then turned out the overhead light and got into bed. "It's okay, love, really. Go to sleep."

She wormed her way under his arm, and soon fell asleep there. Alan lay wide-eyed in the dark, waiting for what might come next. He heard the usual sounds of a house relaxing, but nothing more. Time passed, and the light in the room went through gradations of shadow as the sun rose and tried to peek through the curtains. Still he lay, unmoving, unwilling to disturb his wife as she rested—he couldn't shake the feeling that something was coming. Something wanted to announce itself, and their lives would never be the same.

*

The next few weeks were quiet, for the most part, and Mary almost began to believe that they'd imagined it all. The birth of their daughter wasn't far away now, and life seemed to consist of hospital visits, shopping trips for last-minute 'essentials' such as armloads of nappies, babygros, creams… you name it, they bought it, eager to be fully prepared. In between those trips and spring-cleaning the house to make sure everything was done ahead of time, there hadn't been much time for anything else to intrude. Now, all was finished, and her thoughts began to turn to what it would be like to greet her child. As they pulled into the hospital car park for a final scan, Mary felt the baby *shift*, not so much kicking as turning around entirely, forcing her to stretch out in the car seat, something that wasn't exactly easy.

"You okay?" Alan asked, alarmed.

"Yeah," she answered, sighing. "She's just having a kick around in there, I think." The baby shifted again, and she winced. "Now I need to pee."

Alan grinned, and pulled into a parking space. "Hang on, then. Won't be a minute."

He was true to his word, and five minutes later she let herself into the Ladies and locked herself in a cubicle. Pain lanced through her abdomen, making her cry out—then the baby *lurched*, and Mary passed out. When she came to, she was leaning against the cubicle wall, and her head throbbed. She put her hand to her forehead and it came away bloody. Had she fainted? Gingerly, she stood and looked into the bowl, fearful of what she might see. There was nothing there, and the pain had abated; perhaps all might yet be okay. She heard a murmur of voices outside, and realised Alan was probably out there, worried. How long had she been out? She tidied herself up, washed her hands, and wadded some tissues against the cut on her head. Then she let herself out into the corridor, where Alan stood, concern etched on his face.

"Mary!" He came to her, and looped an arm around her waist, coaxed her hand away from her forehead. "What happened?"

"I fainted, I think," she whispered. "I feel a bit sick."

"Come on," he said. "Let's sit down for a minute." He led her to a chair, and busied himself cleaning the cut on her forehead, then got her a cup of water from the cooler in the corridor. She drank it, then nodded, a little bit of colour returning.

"Thanks, I'm okay now."

"Are you sure?"

She nodded again. "I'm fine. I just got woozy for a sec, that's all, and the next thing I knew I was waking up."

"Well, at least we're in the right place," he said. "Come on, let's get this scan done, and let them know what happened."

*

The scan went without incident, and Mary found herself watching the movements of her baby in wonderment, Alan by her side. The child kicked and turned, and Mary saw her daughter was sucking her thumb. It still didn't seem real, yet within a couple of weeks she'd be here, and they'd be a proper family. Things would never be the same.

The baby turned towards the probe again, and Mary froze as she opened her eyes, seeming to look straight at her. "Can she do that?" Mary asked.

"Do what?" the nurse asked, her attention on whatever it was the scan was telling her.

"Can she open her eyes?"

The nurse looked at the scan more closely, then, her brow furrowed. "I don't think so, dear. Perhaps she was just fretting, eh?"

Mary watched as the baby stirred, then went back to the normal foetal position. Dimly, she could hear a baby crying again, and wondered how close they were to the maternity ward here. "Is everything okay with her?" she asked.

The nurse hummed and ha-ed for a few moments as she went over the results, then nodded. "Looks good to me." She looked at Mary then and smiled. "You'll be able to see for yourself soon." She gestured to Mary's clothes and said, "You can get dressed now, you're all done. The doctor will have these in time for your next clinic appointment."

Mary busied herself getting dressed, while Alan looked at the picture the nurse had given them of their baby. He had a beatific smile on his face, and Mary felt a pang at her misgivings. She was letting her imagination run away with her; the baby was fine.

And it was all theirs.

*

Mary's due date was close now; the baby was only days away. She woke, restless, on the Monday; and lay quiet for a while so that Alan could sleep. After a few minutes she couldn't lie still anymore and got up quietly, careful not to disturb her husband. She wandered into the hall and prowled through the upstairs of the house. Nothing stirred. The cat lay comatose on the hall carpet, purring gently as it slept.

The wind sighed in the eaves, and Mary paused. Something rustled, and she looked behind her. Rags had sprung to her feet and was crouched, fur bristling, hissing at some unseen foe. There was nothing there. The hall was empty, and the only sound was the sighing of the wind, and the distant rumble of Alan's snoring.

The wind grew louder, and Mary heard the creaking start in the bedroom. She whimpered, and told herself it was a draught—the double glazing was faulty, that was all. They'd have to call the builder back and get him to fix it. Alan shifted in his sleep, and moaned, and Mary took an involuntary step forward. She couldn't leave him alone in there. *Squeaaaaak… squeeeeak…* the sound was louder now, more insistent. Mary became aware of a shushing sound, and stopped—she didn't want to go into that room. She didn't want to even be in the house, let alone in the bedroom, but Alan was in there, alone, and she couldn't desert him.

The bedroom door was ajar; had she left it like that? She couldn't remember. She pushed it further open, and stepped inside.

The bedroom was in shadow, save for a shaft of dim light that fell on the cradle from the window. Mary moaned as she saw that the window was different now… the modern glazing was gone, replaced by an old-fashioned sash window; paint peeling and rust patches clustered around the lock. The wind howled through a crack in the glass, and the cradle rocked faster.

Mary's feet moved without conscious instruction, and as she

edged closer she saw a dark shadow squirming in the depths of the cradle. The crying was louder now, and Mary saw a darker shadow open in the midst of where the phantom infant's face must surely be. This was the source of the crying; the cradle bore some remnant of a child that had expired in its midst, the sadness palpable around it now, a cloud of misery that reached out to devour everything around it.

A shadow moved past Mary, and she flinched. She watched as it moved towards the cradle, spectral arms reaching out to pick up the dead child and clutch it to its phantom bosom. Mary saw skeletal fingers clutching at non-existent tresses as the baby wailed and wailed, desperate for comfort that would never come.

She screamed as she felt the first pains, and simultaneously saw the baby's head turn towards her, arms reaching for her, her body responding even as madness closed in.

*

Alan woke, then, and found his wife unconscious on the floor. He leapt from the bed, and struggled to lift her, but finally he got her on the bed. Her breathing was shallow, her expression pallid, and he groaned as he saw the dark stain spreading on the sheets. "Oh Jesus, love," he cried. "You're bleeding. Oh God." He went to pick up the phone, but her hand gripped his wrist, and he saw her eyes flutter open briefly.

"Don't leave me," she pleaded. "Please." Her eyes closed again, and she screamed as another spasm ripped through her.

Alan quickly dialled the emergency services, and called for an ambulance. Details given, he slammed the phone down as she rallied once more, and went to his wife.

"Lean on me, love," he said as he sat beside her on the bed. "Help's coming. Just hold on."

Mary smiled, then; her face so sad as she stroked his face. "She's coming, Alan. Don't let it get her."

Mystified, Alan nodded, and held Mary's hands as she breathed through another contraction. He heard a cry, cut off suddenly, and saw his daughter lying on the sheets even as she breathed her last.

Mary sobbed, and reached out to her baby, then screamed and started batting at the bed. "Get away! Get away from her!"

Alan heard the distant whoop of the ambulance's siren, signifying it had found the lane to their cottage. He ran downstairs and unlocked the front door, leaving it ajar for them—they'd be with him in moments. Then he ran back up the stairs to his wife.

When he opened the door, he stopped in his tracks; unable to process what his eyes insisted he was seeing. Mary was crying, stroking their daughter's lifeless body—and a shadow was reaching out, ushering what looked like a phantom infant towards her still form. He screamed as the shadow-child reached his daughter, and ran forward. The shadow drew back, clutching the long-dead infant to its chest, and vaguely he was aware of Mary shouting "The cradle! Get rid of the cradle!" He rushed over and lifted the cradle, grimacing as it fought in his grip, the spirit of whatever poor soul had lost her baby in the cradle trying to wrest it from him, to be returned to its place by the window. He wrenched it free, and—opening the window as wide as he could—hurled the cradle out into the night. There was a flash as it hit the ground, and he saw, just for a moment, a young woman clad only in a white shift, holding a screaming infant out to him, pleading for her child. "Save her," she sobbed. "Save my baby!"

The ambulance reached them then, the blue light's strobe casting the nightmarish scene in an impossible light. It drove over the cradle—the spirit screamed and was torn to shreds, fingers of mist dissipating in the wind even as the sound was fading, fading. Then the night was still, apart from the normal sounds of the wind, and of the ambulance parking and its crew getting out and coming to the door.

*

The child on the bed mewed and moved, mouth open in a maw of distress as its little arms and legs waved around. The ambulance crew took one look and, while one went to Mary and started to examine her, the other wrapped the infant in a blanket and gave it the once over. Satisfied it was a healthy birth, he offered the child to its father, who was crying in the hall.

"This one's a fighter," he said, smiling. "She wants her mother." He looked back into the bedroom and then held the child tighter. "You can give her to her in a minute."

Alan smiled. "Mary's okay?"

"She's fine, sir. A bit shocked, hysterical, really; but then she's been through a lot." The man smiled at him, then, his expression kindly. "They'll both feel better when Mum can give baby a cuddle."

Alan nodded, and took his daughter from the medic's arms. He looked down at her face, pink and distressed, and took the waving fist in his own. The baby quieted, and he smiled at her as she watched him, curious now rather than afraid. "Come on, little one," he whispered. "Let's go and see Mummy."

Play Time

Tommy stood still, head cocked to one side, listening to the night-time noises of the playground. By day these places were full of the sounds of children squealing with delight, maybe crying at some mishap—a fall, or a bang to the head or knee, perhaps an argument with a friend or a tussle with a bully. But overall playgrounds were happy places, full of joy. Even their name showed that to be true.

Night-time was different. By night the only sound was the wind moaning through the creak of the swing's chains and the whispering of the leaves on the trees—the slow sigh of the night's chill as the playground waited for morning to come and banish the darkness. That was all the noises could be, he decided. He'd listened to, and catalogued, each of these sounds, one by one, until he was satisfied, huddled as small as he could make himself: a small dark shadow on the last swing on the row.

He sighed, wishing it was earlier. There was no-one left to play with—all had gone home for their dinner, full of the day's adventures and ready for sleep to claim them; only to release them in the morning, eager for more. Their mothers had come for them, reducing their number by degrees until he was the only one left. He eased his weight back and kicked off with his feet, letting the swing carry him gently backward—he wasn't sure where his mother was; and it was late. *Shouldn't she be here by now?* his mind whispered, and he told it to shush. *She'll be here. She'll come.*

He tilted his head at a new sound—one unexpected at this hour. There it was again, the high-pitched tinkling of a girl's laughter. He craned his neck to look behind him into the bushes, then scanned the rest of the playground, but could see no-one. Digging his heels into the earth below him, he brought the swing to a standstill, quieting the creak of the chain against the crossbar. A sudden gust of wind whispered through the trees, and errant leaves danced in the air before him. *Tommy…* Now he knew he was imagining things, because the wind couldn't know his name. Footsteps skittered off to his left, and he whirled around to see what was there. The sodium light guttered fitfully, barely illuminating a small circle around it, but it was enough. A shadow was cutting off part of the lit circle—a girl shaped shadow, from what he could see. Boys didn't have pigtails. *Maybe it's not pigtails,* his mind whispered again. *Maybe it's horns!* He whimpered, and this time the laughter wasn't just in his head. It rang throughout the playground, and Tommy saw a light come on in a house behind the park.

"Silly, girls don't have horns."

Tommy gasped—and felt icy fingers play his spine. The voice—and the pigtails, apparently—belonged to the girl standing at the edge of the light, staring at him as if he'd said something stupid. He hadn't, had he? He was only thinking.

The girl grinned at him, then, and he knew, he just knew, that she could hear what he was thinking—even if she said nothing about it.

He took a deep breath before asking, "Who are you?"

"Who do you think I am?"

Tommy frowned. "That's kind of a stupid question," he said. "How am I supposed to know that?"

The girl moved back a little, so that all he could see was her eyes. The rest of her stood in darkness, but her eyes glowed with yellow light, and oh, how they danced.

"I guess that's true." She moved a step closer to him, and the wind screamed. "My name's Mary."

"You're out kind of late, Mary."

"So are you," she retorted, and she inched a step closer, twisting the cloth of her dress in her fists. "Shouldn't your mother have come for you by now?" Her skin was pale, her mouth pinched—she looked so *cold.*

Tommy looked around at the gate on the far side of the playground, and sighed. No one was there. "Yeah, she should." He looked at Mary once more, his face hopeful. "Maybe she got delayed, met someone… you know, got talking." It wouldn't be the first time his mother had been a little late, delayed by another mother who wanted to chat; but it was never more than a few minutes, and she always ran so fast to get to him, so he wouldn't worry. He looked towards the gate once more, hoping he'd see her racing towards him, her red hair flying back in the wind, showing him her relieved smile when she saw him waiting. There was nothing.

"Kinda late, though," Mary offered. Her voice shook, and Tommy wondered just how long she'd been waiting here. "I mean, it's *dark*."

"Yeah, it is," he replied. He took a closer look at the girl, her eyes were huge with fear. "You're not scared… are you?"

"Who, me?" She laughed, but he wasn't convinced. "Nah, not scared." She looked around, seemingly bored, and when her gaze came to rest on Tommy again there was something there that hadn't been before. "You get used to it." Yep, it was there, all right—it was anger, bleeding into her voice more with every second.

"How long have you been here?"

"I don't know." She wouldn't look at him now. "Long time, I guess."

Tommy tried to think if she went to his school. She really didn't look familiar, and it wasn't that big a town. He should know her, if she lived nearby. "Where did you say you live?"

She grinned at him, then; her small teeth almost too white in the darkness. "I didn't." She moved a step closer. "What's the matter, Tommy? Scared?"

"No, I just wonder where she is, that's all." He inched back from her, wary of allowing her too close even while calling himself stupid for letting a girl rattle him like this. "It *is* late."

Mary stood back suddenly, turned and walked towards the roundabout at the edge of the playground. "You're going to freeze if you sit still like that." She started the roundabout turning, pushing at the ground with her foot as if she were on a scooter. "You might as well play while you wait, it'll keep you warm."

Tommy hesitated. His mother would see him clearly while he sat on the swing, he knew… but the roundabout wasn't that far away, was it? She should still see him… and he'd definitely see her. The roundabout squeaked as it turned, and Mary giggled. That decided it. At least if he played with Mary for a while he'd be warm, and—more importantly—he wouldn't be alone any more. He cast one more glance at the gate and then ran to Mary, yelling: "Wait up! I want to play!" The two children laughed as they played, and the darkness crept up and wrapped them up in its embrace.

*

Sarah Warner stood impatiently at the playground gate, trying to stop her hair from getting too messy in the wind. This wasn't the kind of day she'd have picked to go to the park but then her sister wasn't her—that much was painfully obvious. Sarah checked her watch yet again, as if catching the minute hand in the act of moving would magic Lauren into existence.

"What are you doing?"

The voice was unfamiliar, and it took Sarah a moment to realise the words were meant for her. Looking down, she saw a small girl, maybe eight or nine years old, wrapped in a shabby coat and with her socks rolled down around her ankles. One knee was scuffed, but she didn't seem to mind. The girl waited patiently, and Sarah forced herself to be polite. "I'm waiting for my sister."

"Is she coming here to play?"

Sarah suppressed a grin. "No, honey, she's not. We're going shopping."

The girl frowned, thinking hard. Her question, when it came, was so obvious Sarah could have kissed her. "Then why meet here? Is she leaving her kids here to play?"

"No." Sarah didn't want to talk about that. "No, she isn't. She just likes to see kids having fun, I guess." No need to involve this child in the misery of her sister's life; the emptiness.

The child said nothing, just stared at her, and Sarah found herself getting nervous. Why, for God's sake? This was just a kid! Someone called Sarah's name, and both of them looked down the hill—Lauren was bustling towards them, her dark hair unruly and a big smile plastered across her thin face.

"Hi! Who do we have here?"

Sarah didn't know what to say. The little girl looked Lauren up and down, her face serious—Sarah stifled the urge to laugh. Then she grinned, and her face lit up.

"I'm Mary. I was just saying hi." She looked from Lauren to Sarah, and then back to Lauren. "You two don't look much like sisters."

Sarah took Lauren by the arm, not wanting to prolong the hurt for her sister. "No, we don't, but we are." She grinned at Lauren. "Sometimes we even act like it. Come on, hon, time to shop."

Lauren followed her, then turned and waved at the little girl, who grinned and waved back before disappearing into the crowd of children. "Cute kid, huh?"

Sarah searched the playground, but saw no sign of her—she'd melted from view completely. "Yeah, she was great. You hungry?" She urged her sister forward when she nodded, and tried to listen to the prattle—ignoring the feeling that the little girl was still watching them.

*

The clatter of cups on saucers and plates on trays in the heat of the café was almost painful after the quiet of the park in the cold. Sarah felt her face flush in the heat, and managed to get herself out of her coat without having to stand up, which was a relief in this small space. Lauren looked as pale as ever, and Sarah envied the way she never flushed. She took after their mother, pale and dark; while Sarah favoured their father, a man of far ruddier complexion and chestnut hair. She even had his freckles.

The waitress pushed mugs of hot chocolate in front of them, then trudged over to the next customer, already gesturing impatiently. Sarah took a sip of her drink, wiped the foam off her lip, and looked up to see her sister staring at her, deadly serious.

"What's the matter?"

Lauren had the good grace to look abashed. "Another kid went missing last week."

"Another one? Really?"

Lauren nodded, her enthusiasm escaping now she knew she had her sister's ear. "From that playground."

"From the one I met you at this morning?"

Another nod.

Sarah sighed. "Is that why you were so keen to meet there?" Lauren's face fell, and Sarah fought hard to stay kind. She didn't want to frighten her off. "Honey, this isn't healthy."

"What do you mean?"

Exasperated, Sarah blew her fringe out of her way, a habit Lauren knew only too well. Her chin set, as she grew stubborn in return. Sarah sighed. How long was this merry-go-round going to keep running? How many times were they going to end up right back here? "You can't keep obsessing about kids that go missing."

"I'm not obsessing!"

"You're scoping out the playgrounds where they disappear! How is that not obsessed?"

Lauren stared into her mug, her face solemn. A single tear spilled over onto her cheek and cut a track in her make up as it fell. "It's not fair."

Sarah reached for her hand. "No, it's not. And I'm sorry, honey, really I am." She squeezed her sister's hand and handed across a tissue. Lauren ignored her, wiping her eyes and focussing on her cup. "Lauren, kids go missing. All the time. Sad but true."

Lauren glared at her. "That doesn't make it right!"

"No, it doesn't. But it doesn't make them yours, either."

Lauren flinched at that, but Sarah pressed on, hating herself—and hating Lauren for making her do it. "There are ways, Lauren, we've talked about this. Adoption, fostering…"

Lauren was shaking her head, vehement in her refusal to listen. Sarah grew exasperated. "Why on earth would you think hanging around playgrounds is a way to get a kid? It's creepy!"

"I don't know." Lauren's voice was low, choked with grief and self-loathing. "I just like being near them, okay? It makes me feel less…"

"Less what?"

"Redundant. Alone." She glared at her sister now, fierce in her contempt. "I know how that sounds, you don't need to tell me." She wiped her eyes, stared out of the window, at the people wandering by with no idea how hollow her life was. "It just helps."

There was nothing to say, thought Sarah. There were no words that could help here, it was just sad, and raw, and hurtful. And that wouldn't stop anytime soon. She joined her sister in gazing at the world as it passed, blurry in the steamed windows; and perhaps better for it.

*

Lauren sat staring out of her living room later that night, watching the first snow of the winter. The flakes danced out of the sky as if they were bestowing a gift upon the earth—and Lauren thought maybe they were. All the usual ugliness that surrounded them was buried under a pristine, white blanket. Everything was clean and new, just for a little while. She raised her fingers to the glass and traced the shape of a heart, touched her lips to it and smiled.

The smile died, nascent, as tiny, unseen fingers echoed her movements on the outside of the window; leaving icy trails around the outlined heart, setting it hard.

*

The playground looked different tonight. It was colder, thought Tommy, but that wasn't it. The place looked deserted, forlorn—as if kids had stopped coming here. The chains on the swings screamed, and Tommy realised that was because they were rusty. How long had they been here, anyway?

As if called into being, Mary ambled past him into the middle of the playground, her gaze disinterested. "Don't worry about it, they'll come back."

"They will?"

"Sure, they always come back."

Tommy didn't like this. "Why did they leave?"

Mary smiled at him, then, and Tommy cringed. He'd learned to be wary of that smile—the real Mary came out when she smiled, and she wasn't the same. Tommy wasn't even sure if she was a real little girl, when she smiled. He thought that she might be some *thing* that just wanted to play the part of a girl, or even lived inside her. But if there was a thing inside Mary, where was the real Mary?

The girl scowled, her voice rougher this time. Deeper. "I've told you. Best not to worry about that. It's not for you to know." She cuffed him, and he stumbled. "Let's play." He followed her, too scared to say no—wondering, not for the first time, where his mother had gone. And why hadn't she looked for him?

*

Lauren stumbled in the snow, her breath coming in harsh gasps, her lungs burning with the cold. As she trudged up the hill, she searched for the child that must surely be out here. Who else had drawn on her window? Such tiny fingers, they'd die out here if they didn't get warm. Such thoughts buzzed in her head as she homed in on the playground, sure that whoever was lost would find their way here—in the hope that their mother would find them. She hoped that Sarah would find her soon, would help her find whoever was lost. What would she think, when she heard her sister rambling about lost children and icy fingers on her answer phone? She almost laughed, then realised she'd probably given Sarah enough ammunition to make a doctor listen. And then what would she do?

She realised she didn't care. Throughout her life, all she'd wanted was a child and the one time that had been imminent, her chance had been taken away in an instant: her unborn child crushed by the steering wheel of her car as she careened into a wall to avoid an accident. There would be no more chances, not after that. There'd been too much damage, they said. It hadn't taken Dan long to leave after that, although in all fairness a lot of the blame for that lay at her door. She couldn't look at him, knowing what she knew, and he grew tired of promising he didn't blame her and it didn't matter.

Too late now to worry about all that. A cry in the darkness energised her, and she moved forward more purposefully as the park's gate hove into view.

*

Mary turned her head as she pushed her heels into the ground and halted the swing. Tommy, still in mid-swing, followed her lead as soon as he was able. He'd learnt to listen to her, to do as she said. It was less painful that way.

"What is it?" His voice was shrill in the night, his breath plumed out in front of him like Morse code, staccato evidence of his fear.

"She's here." Mary smiled, and stepped off the swing, her mood suddenly light.

"Who's here?"

"You'll see." She was making for the gate, eager to find… what?

Tommy raced after her, not wanting to be left alone. Not here. "Mary, wait!"

She took no notice, just skipped down the path, humming tunelessly as she went. She threw a glance over her shoulder, just once, "Come on, Tommy," and then she was gone. The lights went out suddenly, and he was alone in the dark.

The temperature dropped.

*

Lauren reached the gate, almost sobbing with pain as the cold air burned its way into her lungs. The sound had gone. Just for a moment, she'd thought she heard a cry but then maybe she'd just wanted to. There was more light, suddenly, just by the gate, but Lauren couldn't see where it came from. And there she was. A little girl had stepped into the light, and stood gazing solemnly at her. As Lauren ground to a halt, she smiled, and watched delighted as Lauren sank to her knees.

"You're real," she sobbed.

The little girl nodded, her face wise. "Of course I am. We both are."

"Both?"

Again she nodded, and Lauren became aware of someone standing just behind the girl. A boy, this time. Hadn't she seen his face somewhere before? Recently? He edged forward, his face shy, hopeful. "Do you know my mum?" he asked.

"I'm sorry, love, no. Are you lost?"

"No." The boy grew mournful, and stepped back. He seemed to fade a little. "She is, though. She never came."

The boy's face clicked into place for Lauren then. Tommy Ryan. He'd gone missing from the playground only a week ago, and his mother's body had been found just outside the gates, her throat torn open.

The little girl broke in, cross at no longer being the centre of attention. "She didn't want you, Tommy. Remember? She would have come if she did."

"No, honey, I'm sure that's not true."

"It is!" The girl stamped her foot, and the world darkened. Something grated underfoot and Lauren sat back, stunned. "I told you, Tommy. No one wanted you, just like no one wanted me!"

Tommy's face fell, and as he stared at Lauren she felt her heart break. "Tommy, it wasn't your fault. You have to know that."

The boy shook his head. "Mary's right. If she'd wanted me, she'd have come to find me."

Lauren had to at least try to help him. "Maybe something stopped her."

Mary growled at her, and she recoiled. "Careful, you'll frighten him."

"I just want…"

"To what? Make Tommy think he belongs? He doesn't, any more than I do." Mary took a step closer, and a cruel smile twisted her child-like features. "Any more than you do. You're alone, too, aren't you."

Lauren nodded, bereft.

"They left you, didn't they."

Again, Lauren nodded, dumb with grief.

Mary sidled closer, and Lauren felt a small hand worm its way into her own. She clasped her fingers around it, feeling a warmth grow inside her. "We're alone too."

Lauren looked up at that. "You don't have anyone?"

"Just Tommy." She looked back at him, and he attempted a smile. The effect was repulsive, he looked like he was facing Hell itself. Mary beckoned him closer, and he reluctantly took a step closer, then another. "Tommy and me belong together." She ruffled his hair, and he cringed. His eyes remained locked on Lauren. "Don't we, Tommy?" Tommy said nothing for a moment, then nodded, all hope lost.

Lauren reached for his hand, took it into hers and squeezed. He moaned, and wrapped his arms around her in a hug. He whispered: "Please stay with us. Don't leave me alone with her anymore."

Lauren hugged him tight, tears blinding her. "I won't, I promise."

Lauren's mobile phone shrilled into life, breaking the spell. For a moment she saw Mary as she really was, wizened and old, and needing their warmth to survive. No child, this, rather a creature that might have been a child once, but had been corrupted into this parasitic monster, eager for warmth to keep her here, and for other lives to keep hers going for a little while longer. This creature was hungry, and was prepared to kill to keep her playmate, Lauren saw. The vision of Mary going to Tommy's mother for a hug floated into Lauren's mind, and she cringed as she saw the woman wiping her tears away, and holding her close. Close enough for little teeth to rip into her throat, and tear it wide open.

Mary laughed, softly. "Aren't you going to answer it?"

Lauren stared at the display. It was Sarah. As she clicked the button to take the call, Sarah's voice rose into the night, frantic. "Lauren! Thank God, where are you? Listen…" Lauren dropped the phone, and the tinny notes faded from her mind. She looked at Tommy, and she made up her mind. What did life hold for her, anyway? An empty house and an empty womb, for ever and ever, Amen.

The mobile phone dropped to the ground.

Lauren stood, and took both children's hands. She tried not to cringe from the touch of the little girl, but the child didn't seem to notice. Tommy hung on, pathetically grateful for her affection.

"Come on, kids. Time to go."

Darkness fell, and when the lights came back on they revealed an empty playground, save for a red scarf puddled in the snow; cradling a mobile phone, its volume fading as the battery died.

The sound of children laughing rang in Sarah's ear, as her sister sang a nursery rhyme.

Then they were gone.

In The Howling of the Wind

The old man watched as the child pressed close to the window, staring wide-eyed at the falling snowflakes large and small dancing in the moonlight. He shivered as a sudden draught swept into the room; the door swinging inward as if presaging the arrival of something wondrous.

It was nothing. "Just the wind," he muttered to himself.

The child turned towards him, his eyes full of questions; and the old man felt his spine turn to ice.

"What is it, Grandpa?"

"Nothing… it's nothing, child. Just the wind."

The boy stared at the door, and sighed as it swung shut once more. "Do you think they'll come?"

The old man nodded, clearing his throat as he gestured at the room, the gifts under the tinsel-laden tree, the mantel groaning with cards and pine garlands, complete with golden bells and red velvet bows. "Of course. It's Christmas Eve. Why wouldn't they come?"

The boy said nothing, just stared at his grandfather with an intensity he found unnerving.

The old man leaned forward, tried again. "They're your parents, Matthew, of course they'll come."

This time the boy responded. "How can you be sure?"

"They love you. You are…" he hesitated, suddenly unsure, then continued, "…their flesh. Their blood." He reached out to the boy, who skirted his grasp and hovered just out of reach. "Trust me. They'll be here."

The wind howled as if the skies themselves were in pain, and the boy's gaze shifted to the fireplace, where the wind whispered in sympathy.

"I don't like the sound the wind makes in the chimney."

"What do you mean?"

The boy smiled briefly at him, nervous; aware of how fanciful his words sounded. "It *cries*."

The old man laughed heartily at that. A little *too* heartily. "It's just air, Matthew. Just air." He sat back in his armchair with a sigh and gripped the armrests tightly, taking comfort in feeling the worn fabric under his fingers. On nights like this he drew strength from the feel of the fire warming his skin, the grooves his weight had worn in the chair over the years, the touch of cloth against his body. *This* was what counted, what was real… he cared nothing for what lay beyond the confines of his refuge.

Lights swept across the window suddenly, then were gone. Matthew ran back to the window and pressed his face to the glass. "Grandpa! It's them!" The bell stayed silent, and there were no voices at the door. The boy's smile faded as he surveyed the empty street.

The old man watched as the child raised his hand and laid it flat against the icy pane as if he wanted to melt the ice with its warmth. He called the boy's name, softly, but he didn't answer. He almost didn't hear the boy's sob, muffled as it was by the sudden shriek of wind that battered the house, rattling the windows in their ageing frames.

"Matthew."

The boy said nothing.

"Matthew, come here… Please."

This time the boy came, reluctant, and the old man could see the pain etched on his face. He ached to stroke the child's cheek, hold him close, but that was impossible for a child like Matthew. All he could do was talk to him, and this he did willingly.

"You're a good boy, Matthew. And they love you, even now. If there's a way for them to get here, to get to you, they will."

The boy nodded, but his disbelief shone through. It was in the slump of his shoulders, the way his eyes slid away from his grandfather's, the sorrow on his face. He turned away, and went back to his puzzle, sitting hunched over it on the living room floor.

The old man loved his grandson, always had. Gazing at the

forlorn figure bent over his jigsaw he offered up a silent prayer, *Please God, let them get through.*

*

The chiming of the clock on the mantel woke the old man up, and he heaved himself out of his chair, huffing. Moving around wasn't as easy as it used to be, he found. The clock said it was nine p.m., and the shadows flickering on the walls confirmed the day's passing. The fire crackled in the hearth, and Matthew was still working on his puzzle, his little face solemn but determined. It wasn't natural for a child to be so quiet, he mused. It didn't seem right, although he knew Matthew was perfectly happy, lost in his own little world, where he had always been happiest; never more so than now.

Wandering over to the window, he stared out at the poorly-lit street. Snow had drifted against the walls and hedges, he saw, the parked cars buried almost to the tops of their wheels. The snow on the road itself was pristine, no traffic had disturbed it, and it would be morning, probably, before the gritters reached this far out from town. He sensed the boy's eyes on him and turned, forcing a smile. "The snow's deep, lad, do you think they'll make it?"

Matthew regarded him in silence for a moment. His answer, when it came, was terse. "You're the one who said they would."

"Well, yes, but the snow…"

"You promised." The boy's tone brooked no argument, and the old man sighed, then nodded.

"I did, didn't I. And I meant it, Matthew. If they can make it, they will."

Matthew's smile was singularly humourless, and the old man flinched. "Remember what you said, Grandpa."

"About your parents?"

"About them… and about breaking promises."

The strength drained out of the old man's legs, and he fumbled himself back into his armchair. "What did I say, boy?"

Matthew's smile widened, baring his teeth; his eyes seemed to shine yellow in the firelight, and the old man cursed himself for a fool.

Matthew drew closer, his mouth close to the old man's ear. "You said you must never break a promise. You said God watches."

"God always watches, Matthew, you know that." His voice was thin, quavery, and the boy sniggered as he drew back.

"God's not the only one who watches, Grandpa."

He fought to quell the chill that rose in him at the boy's words. "What do you mean?"

"Others watch, too…" Matthew glanced around, nervous again. "Sometimes I can almost see…"

The wind moaned and whispered in the trees, and the boy's attention was broken. Restless, he returned to the window, and the old man sighed with relief. Matthew had always been such a sunny little child. When had this solemn creature taken his place?

The wind sobbed and moaned in the eaves; this old house was far from well insulated, and it found its way through numerous cracks and gaps with ease. The old man turned his head to the sound, it seemed deeper, somehow, more sonorous. Was that a voice he could hear? The wind seemed to whisper to him, and he fancied he could smell something, a scent that was tantalisingly familiar, but he couldn't place it.

Not yet.

Music wafted down the stairs, a piano tinkling somewhere close by. Matthew stood, and this time his smile was genuine. "Listen, Grandpa. Listen!"

The old man took a step closer to the closed door, flinching as a gust of wind blew it open. The hall was empty, no sign of trespass, just dust motes dancing in the chill night air. Turning back to the boy, he asked, "I almost recognise it, don't you?" He moved towards the door, but hesitated at the threshold to the hall. It was dark out there, the shadows thick and somehow glutinous.

He sensed Matthew, standing just behind him, and moved to take the boy's hand. The boy moved back once more, and the old man sighed. He should have known better. Matthew had never liked to be touched, even before…

"Who is it, Grandpa?" The boy was eager, but not so eager

that he'd come close. The old man yearned for the warmth of a hug from his grandchild, but, as ever, he knew the child wouldn't allow it.

"I'm not sure, Matthew." He glanced back at the front door, dots of white peppering the blackened glass as the snow fell outside in the dark. It was firmly closed. "I didn't hear anyone come in, did you?"

Matthew looked at him strangely, and started up the stairs.

"Come back, boy!" His voice was harsher than he'd intended, and Matthew stopped at once.

The old man moved forward, climbed past Matthew slowly, then continued his ascent. The music faltered, just for a moment, and he froze; gesturing to Matthew to *be still*. He listened to his breath rasping in his throat, his heart stuttering in his chest, and finally the music began again. It was clearer now, and he thought he recognised it. Für Elise. His breath caught in his throat as the memories came thick and fast; how his daughter had loved that melody. One of the earliest tunes she had learnt when she was taking lessons, she had fallen in love with it and played it relentlessly, driving him to distraction even though he loved it. Now it floated down the stairs, bringing images of his beloved girl: Elise drawing, one foot curled beneath her as it always was; Elise at the piano, tongue poking between her lips as she concentrated on her lesson; Elise sleeping, hair spread across her pillow like a little angel…

He wiped a tear from his cheek, and took another step forward, only to freeze when the door at the top of the stairs opened and light spilled out, bathing him and Matthew in a golden glow.

A woman stood silhouetted in the doorway, her features indistinct in the light. Matthew made a move as if to step forward, arms outstretched… and the old man's heart leapt. "Matthew, no!"

Matthew turned to face him, his face wet with tears. "You said she wasn't here! You said we were waiting for them to come!"

"We are, boy, trust me!" Helpless in the face of the child's anger, he struggled for the words to make this right: a way to convince him of the truth.

Matthew's face was all the answer he needed, and it pained him to see so much anger on that sweet face.

The woman at the top of the stairs took a step forward, peering down the darkened hall. The old man stared at her, tears streaming down his face. Why wouldn't she look at them? What more did he have to do?

*

"Mark, is that you?"

As if summoned by his name, the front door blew open and snow blasted through the opening. A tall, dark-haired man rushed through and forced the door shut behind him. As the wind died he took his coat off, but first he shook the snow from his shoulders. He raised his eyes to the woman at the top of the stairs, and his face broke into a smile of such warmth that even the old man couldn't fail to be moved by it.

"Elise!" He stepped forward, raking a hand through the unruly mop that fell over his eyes. "Am I glad to be home! Have you seen the snow?"

The woman laughed, and started down the stairs towards him. "It's coming down fast now, isn't it."

As she reached the bottom he swept her into his arms, holding her tight. Her face was buried against his neck as he asked, "How is he? Is there any change?" Her body stiffened, and he knew the answer even before she shook her head

He held her tighter.

*

Matthew, sitting on a step about halfway up, turned to glare at his grandfather. "Who does he mean?"

The old man shook his head, unsure. "I… I don't know."

"You do, don't you! You *do* know who it is!" The boy ran down the stairs towards his parents, but stopped short of going to them. He turned to his grandfather suddenly, terrified. "But… when did she come in, Grandpa? I didn't hear her, did you?"

"No, Matthew, I didn't." He stared at the couple entwined in the hall, and gasped as the shadows grew deeper, swallowing them whole. They were alone once more. The boy whimpered and ran back to him, cowering by his side but not touching. "I didn't hear a thing."

"Where did they go? Did you see?"

The old man could only shake his head. The house had changed, somehow; the wind carried voices and sounds from things unseen, and the night outside was fierce.

They couldn't leave.

*

Midnight, and the old man woke to find the fire sputtering. Matthew was asleep on the rug before it, curled up in a ball. His beloved puzzle was gone.

The old man stared around the familiar room, wondering how things had changed, and why. Shadows flickered in the dying firelight, and with them, the room… *altered.* There was a painting over on the far wall that he didn't remember, had certainly not bought, it was too modern for his tastes, too *bright.* The television (how he hated the things, had always kept it hidden in a unit that looked like a wooden chest) was displayed proudly, and it was huge, not the smaller model he remembered. The ticking seemed to grow louder, and he turned to stare at the clock on the mantel. It was still there, calling him, but some of the ornaments up there were new, weren't they? There was a photo frame that was unfamiliar, with a bud vase beside it, now empty. He went and stared at the photo, felt the chill of the room sink into him. The figure that stared back was his own, a photo taken by his daughter Elise, on his seventieth birthday. For the life of him he couldn't remember when that had been, and wondered anew if he was going senile. He moved to the window and looked out at a wonderland; the ground was thickly carpeted with fresh snow and the sky was midnight blue, starlight making the snow glow cobalt-white.

There was another photograph on the windowsill, and

he traced the outlines of that familiar face, feeling the chill pervade his body. Matthew. A happy, cheeky Matthew, not the quiet, untouchable shadow he had become. Next to this was a photograph of Elise with her husband, Mark; as yet untouched by the world's harsh reality. These pictures spoke of happy times, and he struggled to remember them… to remember his place in all this. And Matthew's.

He looked back at his chair, and froze. His beloved chair was gone, replaced by something newer, sleeker. He didn't like it. Yet when he closed his eyes and touched this… the familiar cloth sprouted beneath his fingers, only to vanish when he looked again. The smell of smoke made him cough, and for just a moment the heat in the room was intense, then the chill settled in once more.

And what of Matthew? He stared at the sleeping boy, wondering whether to wake him; he knew the child wouldn't react well. He rubbed his eyes, unsure of his vision suddenly; the boy appeared *dimmer*, somehow. Less there. He wondered how many more of these tricks the house would play on him before the night was over.

He stumbled into the hall, lost in this space that, once so familiar, now felt so strange. Music floated downstairs again, and he cried out in fear. Where was she? He made his way quickly up the stairs, eager to see his daughter, have her tell him what was happening.

*

Elise sat on the bed, clasping a picture in her hands, her face wet with tears. A bedside lamp made the tear tracking down her cheek glisten. The old man hovered in the doorway, unwilling suddenly to intrude on this, his daughter's grief. A door on the other side of the bedroom opened, and Mark appeared.

"Elise?"

She smiled up at him, put the photo back on the bedside table. Matthew laughed at her from it, caught in delight at some past party. "I'm sorry. I'm okay, really."

Mark nodded, sympathy evident as he asked, "Can I get you

anything?"

She thought for a moment. "A tea would be nice, if that's okay?"

He grinned at her, then. "Should have known." He crossed to the bed, kissed her on the forehead. "Of course it is. I'll be back in a minute."

He brushed past the old man without acknowledgement, his face set. The good humour was purely for his daughter's benefit. What was wrong, he wondered? Was she ill? He moved closer, silent, unwilling to disturb her now she seemed to be resting.

She lay on the bed, eyes closed, and the old man became aware of the plaintive strains of *Für Elise* once more, the CD player beside the bed set low. He had named her for this song, over her mother's wishes. She had thought it too fanciful, instead of beautiful. He supposed it was lucky she'd loved the tune as much as he did.

He sensed movement beside him, and realised Matthew had joined him at his mother's bedside. The boy stared forlornly, and the old man was saddened to see how pale he was. Elise rolled over, and before he could think what to do, he found himself and the boy back out in the hall, just in time to sink deeper into the shadows as Mark returned.

The hall brightened for a moment as Mark went into the bedroom, then darkened again. Matthew and his grandfather stood just outside the door, listening, a little ashamed of themselves. Elise and Mark thought they were alone, and perhaps that was best, though neither of them could have said why.

*

Mark sat on the edge of the bed, a steaming mug of tea in his hand. He shook his wife gently. "Elise, wake up. Your tea."

She opened her eyes and stared blankly at him for a moment, then smiled and sat up, taking the cup. "I must have drifted off."

"Not surprising, love. You must be exhausted."

Her smile faded as she tried not to cry. "I'll rest when he wakes up."

Mark opened his mouth as if to speak... and then closed it again. This was old ground, gone over too many times already. The wounds were fresh, just under the surface, and he had no wish to open them again.

The phone shrilled, and Elise dropped her cup.

*

Matthew sat on the hearth, his arms wrapped tightly around him. He stared up at his grandfather.

"Where did they go, Grandpa?"

"I don't know, boy." He was staring out of the window, at the tracks their car had left in the snow as it screeched out of the drive. "I don't know."

Matthew wasn't about to give up. "But it's late, the middle of the night. Why didn't they check I was alright, or take me with them?"

The old man could only shake his head. "I suppose because they knew I'd look after you." He sat down heavily, relieved to find the room back as he remembered. "But they should have told us, that's true."

The house was dark, and cold, but neither moved to turn a light on, or lay the fire.

Time passed, shadows fell. And the wind was screaming.

*

Elise stared at the shape in the bed before her, so pale and weak. She could barely take in the doctor's words.

"He's been showing signs of waking, Mrs. Banks. Very slight... but definitely there." A monitor went off again, and nurses bustled, clustering around their patient. He still hadn't moved. She felt a hand rest on her shoulder, and another snake round her waist. She leaned back, grateful for Mark's warmth. He kissed her hair.

"What do you think, Mark? Will he wake up?"

He sighed. "I don't know, darling. But God, I hope so."

"It's been so long…" Elise's voice cracked, and she put a hand to her mouth; desperate to contain her grief.

Mark nodded. "I know."

They looked on, then, as the doctors worked; and they waited and watched, as they had for so long, forlorn in the hope that this time, maybe this time, hope would win.

*

Dawn was breaking through the living room window, its watery rays struggling to illuminate the cold and stark room, where Matthew and his grandfather sat waiting. As the room brightened, Matthew cried out, and his grandfather whirled towards him. The boy was… flickering. The old man watched in shock as the image of the lad faded out of sight. Then he was back, just for a moment… reaching out towards him. With a cry, he made a grab for his grandson's hand, desperate for the contact… and to keep Matthew with him.

Too late.

*

Elise was exhausted. Mark was by her side, and they leant on each other as they searched for some sign of the doctors' success. As dawn broke, Elise called her son's name, her voice shocked. Following the direction of her gaze, Mark saw his son open his eyes briefly, and smile at his mother.

"Matthew!" He was back, suddenly, and the old man slumped with relief. The boy was jittery, frightened… but he was here. "What happened, boy? Where did you go?"

"I don't know." The boy was staring around him, as if he were trying to fix his position, set it in stone. "It was bright… there was a bed… and my mother was there."

The old man wept. "Did she see you?"

"I think so." Matthew's voice shook with emotion, the first real feeling the old man had seen since… when, exactly? "She smiled… I *think* it was at me."

The boy began to fade again, and the old man moaned. "Don't leave me, Matthew. Don't leave me alone."

The boy flickered back into view and smiled. "Don't worry, Grandpa. I won't." He grasped his grandfather's wrist, and the old man cried out at the surge of feeling that shot up his arm.

*

They were back in that room, by the bed, but this time they were together. Matthew stared up at his grandfather, then at the figure in the bed, his face milk-white.

"Grandpa, look!"

The old man obeyed. "I don't understand, Matthew. How can this be?"

Matthew drew closer to the figure, traced the contours of its face, entranced. "I don't understand either. How can it be me, Grandpa?"

*

Back in the house. Alone. The old man groaned as he surveyed the living room he'd loved so much, and he remembered. The heat rose around him as he saw those flames lick the carpet and up the walls, the ember of coal that had caused this carnage glowing innocuously on the floor in the midst of it all.

He saw, again, the Christmas tree going up in flames, the smell of pine pervading the house as if it were no more than a scented candle. He groaned as he saw his beloved chair blacken, then burst into flames, the fumes causing the old man (he recognised himself, and started to cry) to scream in anguish as he rose to his feet and tried to put the flames out, calling out the name of the boy entrusted to his care while his parents were at a party. "Matthew! Matthew!"

He saw the child, huddled on the stairs, coughing; tears tracking through the grime on his face as he called in vain for his grandfather. He saw the hope in his eyes die as he realised no help was coming. Then he saw the boy slump to the floor as the smoke overcame him, eyes closed.

As he watched himself fall to the floor, flesh blackening as the flames licked at his body, he heard the front door as it broke under the force of the fireman's axe. He felt himself smothered, too late, by a blanket as he heard another man's voice call for oxygen: "There's a kid up here! Quick, bring oxygen, he's still alive!" He remembered the feeling of panic as he fought to stay alive. He'd been entrusted with the child, he had to look after his grandson!

Now, as the memories crashed in and he realised, too late, what had happened that fateful night, he heard Matthew calling him; and then he was back by the boy's bed, watching as he woke.

*

"Grandpa?"

Elise was crying, even as she smiled at the boy and shushed him, brushing his hair back off his face just like she had every night since the beginning. Mark watched his wife and son whilst trying not to show that he too wanted nothing more than to break down after the stress of the last months.

Matthew looked beyond them, his body frail and his face wan, but he saw his grandfather. And he smiled.

The doctors were checking the boy over, this child that had hovered for so long in the between spaces, neither dead nor alive. Matthew took no notice. He looked at his grandfather, and he reached out his hand.

The old man reached for the boy's fingers, clasped his hand in his own even though he knew neither of them could really feel it. He tried to explain, to make it right.

"I was supposed to look after you, Matthew."

"You did, Grandpa. It wasn't your fault."

Elise frowned, worried. "What wasn't Grandpa's fault, Matthew?"

"The fire. He thinks he didn't look after me."

Elise shook her head. "The fire was no one's fault, darling. A fluke, that's all. Your grandfather would never intentionally let you get hurt."

Matthew nodded. "I know, but he thinks it was."

"He does?" Mark drew closer, leant over his son. "Can you remember the fire, son? Can you remember anything?" He exchanged glances with his wife, fearful of the answer.

Matthew shook his head. "No, nothing. I was coughing, then it was dark." His face brightened as he did, indeed, remember something. "I remember Grandpa, he's been with me."

"He has?" Eager to soothe the child, and close this chapter, his parents played along. They had no wish to lose him again if he was stressed, they just wanted to forget, and move on.

"All the time," Matthew continued. "He helped me with my puzzle while we waited."

"Waited?"

"For you to come home from the party."

Elise felt Mark's hand tighten on her shoulder. In the months since the party, while they'd buried her father and watched their son as he lay comatose, she'd blamed herself again and again for leaving them; for being out of the house when disaster struck. For leaving them alone. Had her father somehow managed to stay with Matthew, through all this? Had he stayed by his side?

Matthew giggled, and Elise fought to stay calm. "What's funny, sweetheart?"

Matthew's smile was warm, his delight genuine. "Grandpa. He says thank you for not blaming him, now he can go, find peace." Matthew's face fell. "He's leaving."

Mark cleared his throat, amazed at Matthew's words. "He needs to go to Heaven, son. He needs to rest."

"He died?"

Matthew's voice shook, but then the smile returned as his grandfather spoke. "Your place is here, Matthew, with your parents. I can leave you now you're back with them; it's where you belong."

"But where will you go, Grandpa? When will I see you again?"

"I'm going home, son. And I'll always be watching you, never fear." The old man started to fade, and Matthew's face fell. He buried his face against his mother's chest, feeling her wrap her arms around him. His grandfather smiled, and nodded, and pointed out of the window, at the snow. "Go home, Matthew. It's Christmas, and your parents have everything ready, just waiting for you."

Matthew sniffed back a tear as his grandfather faded, and looked up at his parents. "It's Christmas?"

Elise nodded happily. "Yes, it is, Matthew. Tomorrow…" She looked at the clock on the wall, "no, today, in fact."

Matthew grinned, then, and waved at what seemed, to everyone else, to be thin air. "Bye, Grandpa. Bye… and Happy Christmas!"

Sleeping Black

Black hands on white paint.

Seth blinked and rubbed his eyes, groaning. Not again.

Black handprints on the wall opposite the bed, about two feet off the floor, gaps between the pads of each section of the fingers; a larger gap around the black pad and heel of the hand, white spaces in the gaps. As he watched, the finger-marks smeared, as if someone were trying to clean the wall before he woke up.

Too late.

He turned his head and looked across at his wife, Trudy. She was fast asleep; lying flat on her back, mouth wide, snoring for all she was worth. Her eyes were covered by a black satin sleep mask that lay tight against her puffy cheeks, which he'd bought to stop her moaning about the brightness of their bedroom in the mornings. It hadn't stopped her moaning once she was up and about, nothing ever did; but at least she didn't have any excuse for being unable to sleep now. He sighed and rolled out of bed, heading for the bathroom to get a damp cloth and clean the wall before she started to stir. The marks came away easily enough, and he didn't think she'd notice the faint burnt odour, it was already fading, helped along by the lemon cleaning fluid on the cloth. There. It was gone. He straightened up as his wife turned over and sighed, and made his way back to the bathroom to return the cloth before she could ask him what he was up to.

*

They'd been living here for three weeks now, and, too late, he'd realised his mistake. The house was beautiful, there was no doubt about that, left to him by his late grandmother, the last (except for him) of a long line of Wyers; the house had originally come into the Wyer family when it was bought by his great-great-grandfather, who'd owned a firm of sweeps. It sounded so innocuous, he thought, a firm of sweeps. What it meant, of course, was children. Small boys, mostly, that his great-great-grandfather had bought from the workhouse, or 'saved' from life on the streets, and forced to work for him, sending them up chimneys clad in nothing but rags, or nothing at all, to clean them out, with scant regard for whether they lived or died. The Wyer name was notorious in the sweep trade, and Seth had worked hard when starting out to distance himself from that reputation.

Seth wasn't a bad man. At least he didn't think so. He still owned a chimney sweep firm, the same one in fact, but these days all the work was done by machines. No one had to physically climb a chimney and grub about in the dark, terrified of what might fly out at them, or of falling to their deaths. He felt a deep and abiding shame when he thought of how his great-great-grandfather had built the firm; the conditions those children must have lived in, and the cruelty the great man had shown them. Still, those days were long gone. When his grandmother had died, almost a year before, she'd left the house to him in her will. And what a state it had been in. She'd ordered it locked up years before, after concerned relatives had had her committed. She'd been raving about children, and soot, and something coming for her... but no one had believed her. Why would they? She'd been seventy even then, and had been found running down Upper Street in Islington in nothing but a thin white cotton nightdress, screaming. Her head had been bleeding, clumps of her hair still in her clenched fists when the police managed to hold on to her and force her to lie down on a stretcher. "I'm sorry," she'd moaned, tears streaking her blackened cheeks. "I'm so sorry. It wasn't me."

No one ever found out *what* wasn't her, precisely, but Seth thought he knew. When he'd first come to London to see his inheritance, the house had been unprepossessing, to say the least. The windows and doors were boarded up, the boards themselves cracked and swollen, gaps in between letting in God knew what. He'd hired a firm of builders to come in and renovate, but that first day had been all about getting the boards off and seeing what they were dealing with.

Christ, what a mess. The floorboards on all three floors were warped as a result of holes in the roof letting rain and snow in over the years. The whole place was thick with dust, the floors covered with mouse and rat droppings. Bare slats poked through where large areas of plaster had rotted and fallen to the floor; it wasn't even wired for electricity, and had only basic plumbing, a sink and pump tap in the kitchen. There were fireplaces in every bedroom, and in both receptions, a range cooker in the kitchen. All the fireplaces had been boarded up, rough sheets of plywood nailed into the surrounds. It stank of dust and damp and general neglect, and Seth had felt his heart sink as he surveyed the damage in room after room. It was going to cost a fortune to put right.

*

He'd had several meetings after that first visit with the building firm he'd hired, armed with his wife's wish-list (she wasn't going to set foot in that house until it was done, she'd told him; God knows what might be living in the walls, you could get eaten alive). Her list was extensive: en suite bathrooms, chandeliers… Trudy liked the finer things in life, and now they'd inherited a big house in Islington it seemed to Seth that she was having delusions of grandeur. Still, they could afford to splash out, and that house was definitely worth it. It would be a thing of beauty once they'd finished. Seth grinned wryly to himself as he remembered Trudy's name for it: "It'll be our forever home," she'd said. Once, that had sounded wonderful. Now it sounded like a threat.

The workmen had grumbled, of course; that went with the territory, didn't it? It was a big house: four bedrooms, two receptions, a grand hall and massive kitchen. There was even a cellar, though Seth had thought more than twice about just boarding that up. He wasn't a fan of the dark, and that space was almost impenetrable; if you stared down through the door in the kitchen that led to the cellar, you saw nothing, just blackness, ready to swallow you whole.

The first job had been stripping everything back to the slats. The plaster was rotten anyway; ripping it all out had been relatively easy, though not exactly uneventful. One of the younger blokes working on site, Nate, had managed to puncture a lung when a slat he'd been struggling to rip out suddenly came free and whipped back, a sharp end stabbing into and between his ribs, straight into his right lung. A thousand-to-one chance, the doctor had said when they'd got him to Casualty. He'd never heard of an injury like that from just pulling a slat out of a rotten wall.

That was the last they'd seen of Nate; always nervous, he'd refused to come back, saying the house was jinxed. "Good riddance," his boss had said, "shown himself for a coward."

No more was said, but Seth couldn't forget the blood. As the boy lay on the floor, moaning, he'd bled heavily; by the time the ambulance got there, he'd been lying in a pool of the stuff. Funny thing, though. Once Nate had been loaded onto a stretcher and the foreman had sent everyone home for the day (no one was in much of a mood to carry on after that), Seth had come back into the room with a big bucket of soapy water, ready to clean up the mess.

Except there wasn't any. The floor was clean, devoid even of dust. The sweeping marks left by a mop crossed the floor, but it was already dry. Seth wasn't entirely sure how that was possible, but made himself let it go. The foreman must have sent someone back while they were all taking care of Nate, he reasoned. Must have. He took the bucket back into the kitchen and emptied it down the sink, absently listening to the water gurgle down through the pipes to the sewer below. Seth shivered. It sounded like something being digested. He stashed the bucket in a cupboard under the sink and made his way quickly out of the house, aware it was growing darker. Was it that late? By the time he got to the front door he was sweating, and he banged the door harder into the jamb than he'd intended, jumping at the hollow bang it generated. He fumbled in his pocket for the keys and then almost dropped them in his haste to lock the door. He fiddled around for the right key and finally he found it, sighing with relief as he pushed it into the lock and turned. The tumblers clicked into place, and Seth heard a faint rumble. Frowning, he looked around and tried to remember the local geography. Did the Underground run under here?

He turned his back on the door, ignoring the itching sensation between his shoulder blades, and surveyed the quiet street. The house had been dark, and growing darker by the minute; he'd thought sunset must be close. Yet here, outside, it was a sunny mid-afternoon, hours of daylight left. He shook his head and resolved to check the windows; he'd thought all the shutters had been removed, but perhaps the foreman had put some back because of broken glass or something. He turned and stared upward, but saw nothing to suggest that; blind glass stared back at him, absorbing what light it could into the shadows within. He stood there for some minutes, watching, but the house was quiet. Finally, he turned and walked swiftly to his car, eager to get home.

*

The renovation had gone fairly smoothly after that; if he were a superstitious man, Seth thought to himself, he could almost believe that it was satisfied with the blood already spilt. In a matter of six weeks, the plumbing and wiring were in with no injury worse than a stubbed toe or cut finger. The workmen seemed happy, although he'd heard mutterings about this job being jinxed; echoes of Nate on the day he was hurt. "Ignore them," the foreman said, "builders like to moan, you know that."

And he did know that, didn't he. He'd seen enough of it in his lifetime; sweeps weren't averse to a good complaining session either. Still, the job was getting done. Plaster went up and refurbished floorboards went down; the house started to look as if it might make a home again one day.

Seth had wandered into the kitchen early one morning, ready to oversee the installation of the new cupboards and sink. The kitchen was huge, running the entire width of the house at the back, and gave a view of what was going to be a beautiful garden when the landscapers had finished. Right now it was a sea of dirt and rubble, but he had plans that Trudy would love. A deck, for a start, and a pond, she could have those fish she was always on about; what were they again? Koi, that was it. She could have a whole bloody fountain out there if she wanted, he thought, there was space enough.

He heard something rustling behind him, and someone huffing, and turned around. Alan, the foreman, was helping a lad heft what looked like an armload of canvas out of the cellar, soot dropping everywhere onto his nice clean floor. "What's going on?" he asked.

"Sorry, guv," the man answered. He bore a pained expression, as if he'd hurt himself. "These are a bastard to lift, and they've got to come out. No other way, sorry."

"What are they?" Seth asked, moving closer. They smelled burnt, and he stepped back again, not wanting to get dirty himself.

"Canvas sacking, guv," the foreman replied. "Covered in soot, too. There's loads of 'em down there, it's going to take a few trips to get them all up."

The two men were moving in a cloud of soot; it settled around them like ash, and Seth could feel it getting at the back of his throat. He coughed, and moved back once more.

"Oh well," he muttered, "nothing else for it, I guess." He motioned to the two men to carry on, then cried out when something fell from the middle of the stinking heap. "What's that?"

The three of them leant down and examined the object now lying on the kitchen floor. It was a tiny bone, segmented; perhaps a finger, Seth thought.

The workmen dumped the sacks onto the floor and backed off, rubbing their hands against their clothes as if trying to wipe themselves clean. The foreman looked up, his face white behind the patches of soot that spread across his cheeks and forehead. "Better call the police, guv," he said. "That's human, that is."

*

It was indeed human. The police had responded quickly, several of them making their way down into the cellar even as a forensics officer examined the bone on the kitchen floor, picking it up carefully with gloved hands and placing it into a clear plastic bag.

"A finger," the man said, "from a child, I'd say maybe five or six years old, judging from the size. Not much more than that, certainly."

Trudy had gasped at that, and belatedly Seth realised she'd been hovering in the background, waiting for news. "A child?" she whispered, her voice near tears.

They took a moment to digest the information, no one wanting to think about a small child dying down there in the cellar. Had he cried for his mother? Had he even known her?

Finally, Alan broke the silence. "Why was a kid down there?" he asked. "Under those sacks, I mean. What was a kid doing down there?"

Seth cleared his throat. "My great-great grandfather lived in this house," he said. "He ran a group of chimney sweeps."

Alan wasn't getting it. "So?"

Now the forensic officer spoke. "It wasn't like now," he said. "They didn't have machines."

Alan stared blankly at them, seemingly unable, or perhaps unwilling, to understand.

"They used children," the man went on, and turned to Seth for confirmation, his expression vaguely disgusted. "That's right, isn't it?"

Seth nodded. "They did. Small boys, usually." He stared around, gestured at the cellar door. "They would have slept down there, under spare sacking." Now his voice cracked, as he thought about what it must have been like, how scared those children must have been. "There was a name for it," he said, and found he couldn't look at his companions as he went on; and he certainly wasn't going to catch Trudy's eye if he could help it. "They called it sleeping black."

"Christ."

Alan looked as if he was about to be sick, and Seth couldn't blame him. "My great-great grandfather was ruined when the laws protecting child sweeps came in," he said. "And thank God for that. He ended his days destitute; all that was left was this house."

"So, what," Alan said, "you resurrected the family business?"

Trudy snorted. Seth chose to ignore it.

"That's right, except these days it's all done by machine. Much safer."

The men looked at him for a moment, apparently unsure of how they felt about this new phase of the industry. Seth might be blameless, but the industry was built on blood and tears, no matter how far back that was.

"Look," he went on, "I can't help what he did, can I? It's different now, and I run a clean company; my men are happy with their jobs. This house is pretty much all that's left of the old days, and I want to bring it back to what it was, make it great again." He looked around the kitchen, sighed, and added "and my wife will kill me if I don't."

"Too right," she said, and stormed out of the kitchen.

They laughed at that, and the ice was broken. The forensics officer put the bag into a pocket of his overalls, and made for the door. "There'll be officers searching the basement," he said, "just to see if there are any more bones down there, but these are old. My report will show that, barring anything new turning up down there, they'll be done by tonight."

Then he was gone, and the atmosphere in the kitchen suddenly felt warmer. The foreman gestured down at the cellar, where sounds of policemen digging and generally searching the room wafted up to them. "Can't do much down there now, guv," he said, "not till they're done. I could get on with some plastering in the meantime, if you like?"

Seth nodded. "That'll be great, thanks. The cellar can wait a day or two, I suppose."

Something banged in the room beneath their feet, and both men winced.

"Look on the bright side," Alan said. "At least it'll be emptied out for us."

*

Four days later, Seth stood in the centre of the cellar with Alan and shook his head. "Not so empty after all, is it?"

The police had left a load of canvas sacks piled up in one corner of the cellar; there were footprints all over the floor, tracked in the soot that laid over everything. They'd tracked soot all up the stairs into the kitchen and all over the house while they did a cursory search for anything else untoward; the forensics officer they'd seen had indeed confirmed the bones were over a hundred years old, and no more had been found; eventually, they'd called off the search and left Seth and the workmen in peace, but not before they'd ruined the floors and put them back to square one. It had taken Seth and the whole crew an entire day to clean the floors and walls in the main part of the house, and another to patch up minor scrapes in the plaster, the scratches and scuffs on the new wooden floors left by police boots. Now the house was clean again, apart from the cellar.

Seth took a step forward, reached out and grabbed the handle of a broom leaning against the wall. "I guess we'd better get started, eh?"

Alan nodded and picked up his own broom, and the two men started to sweep.

*

Two hours later, the floor was clear, they'd swept it and scooped several dustpans worth of soot, fluff and general filth from the floor. The brooms were now leaning against the outside wall, and both men were contemplating the final hurdle: the pile of sacking left in one corner.

"What do you think?" Seth asked, and gestured towards the narrow windows lining the outside wall. "Can we get them all out through those?"

Alan tilted his head to one side, contemplated the window frames. "Might damage the frames opening the windows," he said, "they don't look like they've been used in years. Still, you were going to replace them anyway, weren't you?"

Seth sighed. "I was," he said. "Maybe not just yet, but I was." He stared forlornly at the glass, already cracked in places. "What the hell," he said, "might as well clear it all in one go, I suppose."

He moved forward and laid hold of the handles at the bottom of the first window. He braced himself, and tugged upward, hard. The window barely moved, but it was a start. He put his back into it, and the second attempt saw the frame shoot up, making the glass rattle in its frame as it slammed up as far as it could. Mercifully, the glass held, and Seth breathed out slowly, relieved. "Might be able to wait a while after all," he said, and grinned. "Come on."

*

Finally, the cellar was empty, the floors swept. It looked huge, now that everything was cleared away, and Seth found himself wondering what he could do with it. Cinema room, he wondered? Games room? His musings were interrupted by Alan, who walked back into the cellar wiping his hands on his overalls, grinning widely. Halfway through clearing the sacks they'd found a door leading outside, and the job had gone quicker after that.

"All done, guv," he said, "something like forty canvas sacks piled high in one corner against the back wall. I'll take 'em to the tip tomorrow for you, get 'em out of the way."

He looked pointedly at his watch, and Seth belatedly realised how late it must be; the sun was already sinking down below the rooftops, throwing the cellar into a deep gloom. The temperature was dropping fast now that there was no direct sunlight (not that it ever got much), and there was something more, the atmosphere was changing as the light dimmed, and Seth found he didn't want to be in there anymore.

He forced himself to return Alan's grin, and shook the man's hand. "Great stuff, we've done a lot today. Off you go home, have a pint on me, eh?" He followed the man out of the cellar, the skin at the back of his neck itching as if something was crawling there. He slapped at it, his meaty hand raising nothing more than sweat. It was cold down there, he thought, why was he still sweating?

They reached the top of the stairs and he slammed the door shut behind him, turning the key in the lock and stepping back almost in one move.

"What's the matter?" Alan asked.

Seth felt himself redden, ashamed suddenly of the fear that had overtaken him. "Nothing, just want to let you out, lock up, that's all."

Alan said nothing more, but Seth hadn't been convincing, he could see. Still, he was the boss, and if he wanted to hurry up, he was under no obligation to explain himself. He muttered a goodnight and locked the front door behind his foreman, watching through the spyhole in the front door as the man tripped easily down the front steps and made for his car, parked a couple of doors away.

Then Alan was gone, and Seth found himself alone in that huge, empty house. And he realised with something like shock that he hated it.

*

Work went on without any further hitches, and Seth had to admit that was at least keeping Trudy quiet. They already had a nice house, a four bedroom detached in leafy Cuffley, but that wasn't good enough now she knew there was a four bedroom house in Islington they could have. That was proper posh, she said. That was class. Seth smiled to himself when he remembered that. She wouldn't know class if it jumped up and bit her, any more than he would, when it came right down to it. He hadn't lied when he told Alan and the forensics officer that all that was left of his great-great-grandfather's business was the house; he'd grown up working class and hadn't had a problem with that, but Trudy had always wanted more. She deserved better, she said, and in those days—when he'd been blinded by her looks—he'd been happy to work his arse off to give it to her. Except it had never quite been enough; there was always something for her to moan about. Until now, that was. If he could get this house the way she wanted it, he hoped she'd finally be happy, and he tried very hard to ignore the voice inside his head that laughed at that, that asked him if he actually knew his wife.

Then it was moving day, and Trudy was happy. The house

was decorated as she'd wanted, she had her en suites and her chandeliers (all of which she'd been allowed to choose), she'd chosen all the furniture new, rather than bringing anything from home.

Home. Seth looked around at the living room, the huge plump sofas, the carpet you could drown in, the chandeliers… this was home now, for better or worse, and he knew if he valued his sanity he'd better not admit that, actually, he'd preferred their house in Cuffley. Trudy was beaming at him from the other sofa, feet up, fluffy slippers on the carpet at her feet, remote in her hand as she flicked through channels on the obscenely large flat screen TV.

"Comfy?" she asked, popping a chocolate into her mouth.

He nodded and smiled, slightly queasy at the smear of chocolate beside her lip, the sounds she made as she chewed and swallowed.

"Tea?"

He nodded again. "Please."

Then she was gone, off to make yet another cuppa in that enormous kitchen she was so happy with. He heard the distant sounds of the fridge door opening and closing, the kettle being plugged in, and Trudy humming to herself as she pottered about. It wouldn't last. She'd never been particularly domesticated: this was just another new toy to play with till she got bored.

Something nearby rustled, and Seth stiffened. He sat there, barely breathing, listening. For long seconds, there was nothing, and then it came again. It was a soft, rustling sound, as if something were skittering around the floor. Seth leaned forward, searching for the source of the scuffling, but could see nothing. He heard it again, and as he listened, he realised it was coming from the fireplace.

He frowned. He'd had his blokes unblock all the fireplaces and sweep the chimneys clean; there shouldn't be anything in there. He got up and went over to the fireplace, picked up an iron and poked about in the grate. Nothing.

Trudy came back in and glared at him, quick to read his mood. "What now?"

"Nothing," he said. "Just thought I heard something, that's all."

"What?" she asked. "A mouse? Was it a mouse? Oh God, we've got mice, haven't we…"

"We haven't got mice!" he shouted, then managed to measure his tone. "There's nothing here, I've checked. I must have dropped off, imagined it or something."

"Well," Trudy said, "it wouldn't be the first time, I suppose."

She wasn't convinced, and Seth knew she'd be furious if there did prove to be some kind of infestation and she had to have the house fumigated. "I'll get someone in to check it out, alright?" he said. "Just to make sure."

Trudy humphed, but put his tea down and laid a plate of biscuits down beside it on the coffee table. "Don't let it go cold," she warned, which was as close to admitting he'd succeeded in mollifying her as she was ever prepared to go.

"I won't," he said, and sat back down armed with a digestive. "I'll call them in the morning."

Trudy subsided back onto the sofa, slightly out of breath. "I'll have to do more exercise," she said. "I'm puffed." She picked up another chocolate, examining it closely with something that Seth thought looked suspiciously like love. "I don't want to get fat, do I," she said.

He smothered a laugh. "No," he said. "'Course not."

That ship had sailed a long time ago, but he knew better than to fall into that particular trap.

*

The night had passed without further incident and now, here he was, two in the morning and lying flat on his back staring at the ceiling. He could hear a child crying. He wondered idly which house it was coming from, which of the neighbours had a family… and then, as time went on and the crying persisted, he grew angry at whoever it was that could ignore a kiddie who was obviously upset.

At some point he fell asleep, and when he woke the house

was quiet. Trudy had left a note on the kitchen table that filled him with dread: 'Gone shopping.' He made himself some tea and toast and went through into his office, sat down at the computer screen and logged on, checked what bookings the company had coming up. He relaxed a bit when he saw they were fully booked for the next six weeks; most of the bookings were houses in the posher parts of London, a few were small companies in the area. Work was fine for now.

He turned his chair around and gazed out of the window at the street beyond, watched as the neighbours and passers-by walked in either direction, saw various cars come and go. After half an hour or so, he frowned. He'd seen the neighbours on either side leave, the occupants of the house on their left had left together; a middle-aged couple and a teenage girl, sulky at having to go out with the parents. The house on the right would seem to be occupied by an elderly man, and judging by the cars parked outside, no one had small children. No one had child car seats installed, he saw no sign of buggies being loaded into boots, so who'd been crying?

When Trudy came home that night, laden with bags, he asked if she'd got to know any of the neighbours yet. He declined to mention the bags; he valued his life.

"Not really," she said, busying herself with the joy of unpacking. "They all seem a bit stuck up to me, you know?"

He did know. And he could have told her she wouldn't fit in if she'd asked him, but she'd wanted this house and now she had it. She'd just have to learn to like it. "Any kids around here?" he asked, trying to keep his tone nonchalant.

"No, thank God. Noisy little bleeders."

He smiled. She could try and be as classy as she liked, but he knew his wife.

"Why do you want to know?" she asked, looking up from the shopping.

"Just wondered," he said. "Thought I heard one crying last night."

Trudy shook her head. "Nah. Must have been a cat or something."

"Suppose so," he said, oddly relieved. "Hope it doesn't make a habit of it."

*

He'd heard the crying intermittently since then, and knew it couldn't be a cat. Cats didn't call for help, or say they were frightened. And they didn't leave sooty handprints all over the wall. He'd got used to rising early, cleaning the evidence away before Trudy woke up; she'd heard the cat a few times, she said, and had taken to knocking back a couple of glasses of wine before going to bed. So she could sleep. He didn't mind; let her enjoy herself. He had a feeling the house was only warming up.

So now he was sitting in the chair at the end of the bed, watching the wall as Trudy slept. He'd got rid of the latest lot of marks, even though the ghost he now believed it to be had smeared them as he rose, apparently trying to grind the dirt into the wall so that he couldn't clean it. He'd lost weight over the last few weeks, and his pyjamas were baggy now; nothing had been baggy on him in years, and it was only a matter of time before Trudy noticed that, too.

As if summoned by that thought, he heard her sit up. "What's up, you sick?"

"No, I'm fine," he lied. "Couldn't sleep, that's all. Didn't want to disturb you."

Trudy heaved herself off the mattress and came over to stand beside his chair. Her hand, when it felt his cheek, was surprisingly tender, and he felt tears pricking.

"You sure?" she asked. "You're getting a bit thin, Seth."

He smiled. "Yeah, I know," he said. "Diet."

She stared at him for a while, thinking about that, and he could see the wheels turning as she decided whether or not to call him out on his lie.

"Well," she said finally, "don't go too far, eh? Otherwise it's the doc's for you."

"I won't," he promised, and did his best to smile. "Want to go out for dinner tonight?"

"Yeah," she answered, and smiled back, true warmth in her expression for what felt like the first time in months. "That'll be nice. Fatten you up a bit, eh?"

He nodded and smiled, let her wander off to the bathroom. "I'll book a table at that new Italian down the road," she threw over her shoulder. "That alright?"

"Fine," he called, and went back to watching the wall.

*

Dinner had been a great success. Trudy had dressed up, and had even gone out and bought him a new suit. "Other one's too big," she said. "Can't have you showing me up."

She'd worked out his size perfectly, just by looking at him, and he felt much better once he was suited and booted and was sitting down with a glass of wine and a dirty great steak. Good times. Trudy could moan, and did, but she knew her husband, and she knew how to cheer him up when he needed it.

They'd laughed and joked, and worked their way through three courses and a couple of bottles of wine before weaving up the road home and to bed. More good times. Then he'd passed out, happy and sated, and all thought of ghosts forgotten.

That night an explosion of soot burst into their bedroom, apparently let loose by a bird trapped in the flue. Seth didn't know where it could have come from; he'd had them all professionally cleaned before they moved in.

The bird, whatever it was (pigeon?), was flapping about in the middle of a pool of soot, one wing broken, crying its heart out as it tried to escape. Trudy had screamed when it happened, then started crying and decamped to the spare room, insisting she was going to stay there till it was fixed and all cleaned up. When she slammed the door to the spare room, the chimney had puffed out another cloud of soot, and Seth had groaned at what it contained.

A little boy stood in front of him; a little boy maybe five years old, wearing nothing but a pair of britches, every bone in his torso standing out in stark relief. There were huge circles under his eyes, and his cheek bones jutted out above deep hollows. The child was crying and reaching out to him, and Seth felt the room start to spin when he realised the boy was missing a finger.

"It's alright," he whispered, and the boy's sobs started to taper off, his chest hitching as he tried not to cry.

"I won't hurt you," Seth whispered again, and he sighed with relief as the child started to dim.

It was dawn, and as the light in the room brightened the child started to fade, but not before he left his mark. Black hands on white paint, dotted all over the room.

Seth cleaned all the handprints off the wall, then went and phoned Mick, the most trusted of his sweeps. He explained what had happened, and waited for Mick to come and sort it out.

*

Two hours later, Mick emerged from the fireplace covered in soot, echoing the child Seth had seen in the dawn light. "There was a pocket up there," he said. "Some soot had got trapped in it; looks like it all got dislodged when the bird panicked."

He had something in his hands, and now he raised them, holding whatever it was out to Seth. "You'd better get the cops back in," he said. "I found this up there."

"This" was a skull, very small, almost devoid of teeth.

Seth gasped. "There was a kid up there?"

Mick nodded. "I brought this down; the rest's still up there. Thought the police would want it left."

Seth nodded. "Yeah, you did right, Mick. Thank you." He paid the man and called the police, then went to tell his wife.

"There's a what?" she screamed. "In the fucking chimney?"

Seth nodded. "The police are coming," he said, "and Mick's cleaned out all the soot. I'll get the cleaners in once the police take the remains away."

"Remains!" she shrieked. "Oh my God. I can't stay here, Seth. I can't." She was up and flitting about the room, picking up clothes as she went. "I'm going back to Cuffley," she said. "I'll stay there for a few days, okay?"

Seth nodded, dumbly. "Want me to come?"

Trudy stopped what she was doing and stared at her husband. "No," she said, but her tone wasn't unkind. "You stay here and sort things out, love. I don't know if I can live in this house after this." She paused. "Is that bad?"

Seth stared back at her. "What do you want me to do?"

"I don't know. Sell it?"

Seth tried to make sense of what she was saying, but failed. This was the house she'd declared she always wanted. He'd made it perfect for her, just like she wanted. And now she didn't know if she wanted it anymore?

Trudy moved closer; as always, she knew what he was thinking. "I just need to think," she said. "Maybe we could get it blessed or something? What do you think?"

Seth's eyes slowly focussed on her face. Her smug face. "I think," he said, "this is crazy. It's over a hundred years old, and it'll be gone by tomorrow. Call a fucking priest to bless the house if you want, Trude, but I'm not selling. Not after all this."

"Right," she answered, trying to salvage something from the mess. "We'll do that, then. Talk about the rest of it later." Then she swept past him, bag in hand, and clattered down the stairs, leaving him alone once more.

The police had turned up, taken the skeleton away, and when it was confirmed the remains were as old as the finger they'd found, they'd allowed him to finish cleaning the house, putting it right.

Seth hadn't heard the crying since; he supposed the little lad had no need now he was finally found, finally going to be buried. The police were trawling through records from that time, trying to work out who he was, but it was a needle in a haystack, and they all knew it.

The house felt different. It felt lonely. Seth had talked to Trudy a few times in the days since the body was found, but she wasn't ready to come back. "It doesn't feel right," she'd said. So that was that. He'd leave her in Cuffley for a bit; see how things settled. He might even move back there, rent the house out or sell it.

Saturday night, and he was alone. He'd got used to hearing things in this house, whispers and scuffling. He supposed it was haunted by more than one kid after all this time. He thought of his great-great-grandfather and realised he hated him. "All your fault," he slurred, draining his wine glass and reaching for the bottle. "Bastard. Why couldn't you treat 'em right, eh? Why couldn't you feed the poor little sods, look after 'em?"

No answer. Nor had he expected one. The house was cold, and Seth shivered. "Time for bed," he muttered, and drained his glass one last time, shaking the bottle to make sure it was empty before putting it back on the coffee table. "Get warm," he said, barely making sense even to himself. He stumbled up the stairs, stopping twice on the way up to look behind him; to make sure nothing was following. Finally, he reached his bedroom and walked in, then made sure the window was locked and there was nothing up the chimney or in the en suite before he collapsed on top of the bed fully dressed, asleep almost before he hit the mattress.

*

Trudy let herself in and stood in the hall, listening. The house was silent. She'd been ringing Seth all morning, ready to come home. She felt bad about leaving him there, all alone, but if she knew him he was consoling himself with booze and takeaways. She peeked into the living room through the open door and smiled; empty pizza cartons and wine bottles littered the room, it stank of stale food and alcohol. She made her way to the window and pulled the top of it down, keen to let the room begin to air. Then she made her way upstairs, calling Seth as she went.

When she reached their room, she hesitated, scared suddenly to open the door. *Don't be stupid, Trude*, she told herself. *He's just passed out, that's all. Not the first time.*

But she still couldn't open it. She took hold of the handle, and found herself trying not to cry. She felt so lonely, all of a sudden. Why was that? The air was cold, and she watched her breath furl out in front of her as she shivered. Had he left the window open all night? She steeled herself and turned the handle, finally, pushed the bedroom door open and walked in.

And started to scream.

Seth was lying on the bed, face down, and Trudy could see soot all over him. It had blocked his mouth, his nose, and was pooling on the bedspread around both. His face was black with it, and his eyes... his eyes were staring at her, stretched wide, terrified. Someone had laid canvas sacking over his body, lots of it, and she could see it moving as if someone else were sleeping there, using her husband's corpse to keep warm. The sacking was old, deeply impregnated with soot, black as night. Little hands, barely more than bone, crept over the sacking's edge, and Trudy found herself running, screaming at the top of her voice. She didn't want to see. She didn't want to know what was in there with her husband, sleeping black.

Suicide Bridge

He had set out to die tonight, only when it came right down to it, he wasn't sure he could. It was much harder, out here on the ledge.

He shivered violently as the wind rocked him, threatening to knock him off his narrow perch. He drew his jacket tighter around him and bared his teeth in a fierce grin, the cold was the least of his worries. He leaned over for another look.

Traffic streamed by below him, oblivious to his presence. The wind sucked at him, and he leaned as far back as he could, shaking.

Throwing himself off Suicide Bridge had seemed so poetic. After all, that was how it got its name, wasn't it? He took a deep breath, trying to steady himself. Maybe it wouldn't be that bad. He probably wouldn't even know much about it.

He dragged himself to his feet and stood shuddering against the parapet of the bridge. He peered over the edge and swallowed hard against the sudden taste of vomit at the back of his throat. Tears tracked icily down his cheeks as he realised he couldn't do it. Not yet, anyway.

"It's cold tonight."

"What?" He whipped round, and that simple reflex nearly accomplished what all his resolve so far had failed to do. He flailed his arms wildly, instinctively trying to save himself. Then he managed to recover a little, and hurled himself back once more.

"The wind's strong tonight."

Her voice was oddly muffled, as if the wind had whipped it away. She stood a few feet away, leaning back against the bridge. The wind forced her golden hair straight back, exposing every inch of her bloodless face. Even though it was nearly Christmas, a thin summer dress was plastered against her, forcing every curve into sharp relief, yet she didn't appear to feel the cold.

"What's your name?"

"John. John Smith."

She giggled, delighted. "Is it really? I didn't think that there actually were people called that."

"'Fraid so." He had always told everyone that his parents had called him that as some sort of protest against bureaucracy. He didn't like to admit, even to himself, that they were just so dull that they couldn't see the invisibility they were saddling him with. "What's your name?"

"Sarah. Sarah Ryan."

Niceties over, silence blanketed them again. He stood; content just to watch the night for now.

"What are you doing up here, John?"

"What does it look like, Sarah?" She took no notice of his sarcasm, just sat on the edge and let her legs dangle over, as if she was sitting on the end of a pier. The wind ripped into him again, and he shuddered.

Gingerly, he inched towards her perch, and manoeuvred himself into a sitting position beside her. He set his gaze firmly on the horizon, the night lights of London. He'd had enough of looking down for now.

"I'm sorry. I…"

"Forget it." She cut the apology off quickly and smoothly, as if it were irrelevant. "It won't solve anything, you know." Taken aback, he struggled for the right words.

"Maybe, maybe not. At least it'll be over."

The laugh that came back was brittle and surprisingly cynical. "I wouldn't be so sure."

"Oh, I get it. Isn't this where you start your pitch?"

"Pitch?"

"You know, to save my soul." Now it was his turn to be cynical. "I'll bet you want to take me somewhere 'friendly' for a nice cup of tea and a chat."

"Oh, please! Do I look like I've been born again?"

He shook his head, smiling in spite of himself. What she looked like was a girl with a habit, pale and oddly wasted. It didn't matter, anyway. All that really mattered was that all his pleas, his promises of devotion, had turned to dust when Angie slammed the door behind her.

Game over. No more chances.

"Life isn't looking too rosy at the moment, Sarah, I have to tell you." His voice choked as the weight of his tears lodged firmly in his throat. He would not cry. He wouldn't give her the satisfaction.

"Oh, really? Well, from where I sit, it's a hell of a lot better than the alternative!" She was furious, teeth bared in a snarl. Her face flickered, and then she let the mask slip. John flinched, and started to fall. He grabbed desperately for the ledge, and winced at the pain as his wrist was seized in a grip so cold it burned.

Her face came closer to his and he cringed. He could see her skull. He could even see the flattening on one side, with cracks radiating out from what must have been the point of impact. Her face, eerily transparent, was superimposed on it.

"You want me to let go, John? You still think it's such an attractive choice?"

"Please, God…"

"You're praying now? What are you praying for?"

He couldn't speak. He shook his head, tears streaming down his face, freezing his cheeks.

"You want to be saved? Is that it?"

He couldn't answer.

"What do you say? You want to go back to the way it was and forget this ever happened?"

He nodded his head, beaten.

"I guess I don't look so good anymore, do I?"

In spite of himself, he looked up, surprised by the pain in her voice. She took his breath away.

Stripped of all artifice, it was ironic that what shone through the death mask before him was a lust for life. She showed a wild, savage beauty that he sensed could be terrible.

He thought it might even kill.

There was no need to lie as he replied. "You look fine, Sarah. Just fine."

He let her pull him back up

"Are you an angel, Sarah?"

A muffled laugh distracted him, and he peered into the shadows. Then Sarah laughed, and he flushed as the sound of her mirth was echoed by the other figures now becoming visible along the bridge.

"No, John. No angel."

John saw an old man, shabbily dressed, a few steps away. There was a young couple; arms slung casually around each other in a way that spoke of long association. He wondered what could have been so bad that they'd felt a suicide pact was the only way out. Or the old man. At first glance he looked like a hundred other tramps, grubby and defeated. Then he turned to look at John, and a gleam of white caught his eye.

A priest's collar.

"You mean this is it? You're..."

She shushed him then. In his heart the answer lay like a stone, as he supposed it had since the beginning.

"We're nothing, John. We abide, that's all."

"You can't be nothing!" He couldn't bring himself to believe that was all there was. "How can you be nothing? I see you, I hear you." He reached out, pushed a stray lock of hair off her face. "I can even touch you."

She gripped his hand and held it to her face, just for a moment, as if cherishing the warmth. Then she sighed, and released her grip.

"This is it. This is all there is. Always. Sitting here, watching the world go by."

"You don't go on?"

"On to where? Heaven?" She snorted with laughter. "If there is a heaven, John, it's not for the likes of us."

"Don't you know anything, boy? Suicide is a mortal sin." The old man butted in, his voice surprisingly rich and sonorous given his general air of dilapidation. He leaned forward suddenly, and John flinched from the air of corruption that surrounded him up close. He hadn't been an innocent in life, John thought. Not even close.

"But the good you must have done."

"What, because I was a priest? Let's just say the scales were a little wobbly at best. My death weighted the scales firmly against me." He turned away, and John was relieved to have been dismissed.

"Never mind him." Sarah's voice dragged his attention back to her. "You should get out of here, John. You don't belong here. Go home."

"To an empty flat? No job? No… no life?"

"So you lost your job! Big deal. You're not the first and you won't be the last!"

Stung by the scorn in her voice John blurted out the heart of it.

"It's not just the job. It's everything. My girlfriend's pregnant."

"And the prospect of impending fatherhood was more than you could cope with, was it?"

"It's not like that. She doesn't want me to be involved, says I'd make a lousy father." John hung his head, bitterly. "Who knows, maybe she's right."

There was a silence when he finished. It sounded pathetic when he said it like that. People broke up every day; they moved on, they got on with their lives. Not many of them felt as if suicide was the only way out.

Their relationship, though, had been anything but mundane. Tempestuous would have been a better word for it. They had gone from one row to another, punctuated by passionate, though drunken, reconciliations. He'd been too busy getting drunk to notice that she wasn't matching him drink for drink any more. He had just got more self-involved, more maudlin. He'd lost his favourite drinking partner, and suddenly there was no sex at all, passionate or pedestrian.

Then she had told him.

He supposed that the final straw had been when he suggested that the pregnancy need not be a problem. There had been a moment of stunned silence, then she'd said:

"Tell me you don't mean you want me to have an abortion."

"It's not like we couldn't have another one when we're ready."

"When we're ready? What makes you think you'll ever be

ready?" She'd started flinging her things in a bag, crying. "I'll tell you what, I'll make it easy for you. I'll take care of it myself."

Then she was gone.

For a while he hadn't believed that she was really gone. He'd sat there, watching the TV blankly, waiting for the sound of the key in the lock. There had, after all, been many other rows. She had walked out loads of times. So had he. They had never lasted long.

When the door finally did burst open it wasn't Angie, but her brothers. They wasted no time in telling him exactly what they thought of him as they went through the flat packing everything that they could find belonging to their sister. When they'd gone, there was no sign that anyone else had ever lived there with him. They had refused to tell him where she was, or even to pass on any messages. He got the feeling that the only reason they weren't beating him to a bloody pulp was because of some promise extracted by Angie. He supposed he had to thank her for that much, at least.

The next few days had been a haze, when he had only left the flat long enough to reach the off-license on the corner. He had got more and more depressed, and had ended up here, on the bridge; although he had no clear memory of how he had got here.

"John."

"Mmm?"

"Go back to her, John." Sarah's voice broke gently into his misery.

"I can't."

"Give her time. Be the doting daddy when the baby comes. She'll come round, in time."

Now it was John's turn to laugh. "Oh, Sarah, I don't think that's on the cards. It's not exactly in her nature."

"What isn't?"

"Forgiveness." He thought back, dredged through his memories. He remembered her at parties, wild and ecstatic. He remembered her hungriness in bed, her need to dominate. Those were the good times. But there were plenty of bad times, too. The times when she'd shrieked abuse for some imagined infidelity, while she smashed plates and threw anything within reach at him.

After those times, she would get depressed; sometimes even try to harm herself. One memory in particular stood out: the death of her grandmother. From the day she'd died to the day of the funeral, Angie never cried. When they got back from the crematorium she had locked herself in the bathroom. After a while, John had got nervous and forced the door open, only to find Angie lying semiconscious in a tub that looked like it was full of pure blood. Her wrists had gaped like open mouths.

He had raced her to the hospital, and sat and waited. Shortly after, her family had descended on the hospital like a plague, effectively shutting him out. As soon as they could, they had whisked her off to the safety of the family nest. She had been ensconced in her childhood room, complete with fluffy toys and pink wallpaper, something he had always found vaguely distasteful given that she was twenty-five. No one had even bothered to ask what he thought. What he felt.

He had tried not to mind. He had sat at home and waited, phoned dutifully, and she had come home in her own time, just as he had known she would.

Just as he knew this time she wouldn't. Not while there was a baby coming between them.

"Do you really want to end up here, John? Loitering around the scene of your death with all the other suicides, watching the world go by?"

"It might not be so bad. I like the company."

"What's this, John? Flirting with a corpse?" She watched him warily, quizzically, and he had to smile. The situation he found himself in was ludicrous. There was a growing conviction inside him that he had finally found where he belonged.

Sarah already seemed to understand him far better than Angie ever had. He looked up at her, seeking confirmation. She was still keeping her distance, but he thought he sensed her drawing closer. He needed to know.

"Is flirting with a corpse so bad?"

"I don't know. It depends on your perspective, I suppose."

They both smiled then, and John realised he felt at peace.

Sometime during their little exchange he had come to his decision; and whether it was right or wrong, he would have to take the consequences.

"Will it hurt much?"

"Yes. It hurts like hell, I won't lie to you." She seemed to fade, as if unwilling to witness the final step. So he was alone once more.

He hauled himself up, carefully, on legs that were stiff and frozen. Even though he knew it was ridiculous, he didn't want to slip.

He took a deep breath and peered over the edge at the traffic. There weren't so many cars now. The night wind snatched greedily at his clothes. Looking at his watch, he saw that it was nearly midnight. All that time, and no one had missed him.

A bus rounded the corner and started up the hill towards him. If he could time his fall just right, it should do the job quickly and cleanly. He was dimly aware of Sarah's voice, making one final effort. "What about Angie, John? What about your son?"

So it would be a boy. It made no difference now, anyway. They'd be better off without him, safe with her family.

The bus was quite close. The driver was going as fast as he decently could, obviously trying to make up lost time. Perfect. John raised his arms high above his head, took a deep breath, and let himself fall forward in a perfect swan dive.

The frozen air whipping past him seemed almost to be holding him aloft; his fall seemed to take forever. He was glad. It gave him the chance to savour the moment, experience the pleasure of flying. He could see a couple of people at the bus stop just below the bridge; the man's arm came up, pointing, his mouth a perfect "O" of surprise. The woman's hands flew up in front of her face, shielding her sight. Looking back at the bus, he was in time to see the shock on the driver's face as he realised what was about to happen. John smiled beatifically at him. Then he hit the ground.

The pain was immense. He felt it flaring in a million separate places as the wheels tore over him.

Then it went blessedly dark.

He wasn't quite sure how long it was before awareness came

back. It just seemed like one minute he was falling, and then he was back on the bridge

He could see the crowd gathering below. Ambulance lights were already flashing, and darkness had finally fallen, lending everything a weird, strobe-like quality. Police were cordoning off the area, shooing back the crowd and redirecting the traffic while the firemen hosed everything off.

In the middle of it all he could see himself staring blindly upwards, oblivious to the paramedic's ministrations.

He felt sick, suddenly, and he forced his gaze away, focussing on the night sky instead.

"Not very pleasant, is it?"

So she was back. "No." She sat a little way off, still in her summer dress. He realised belatedly that the cold made no difference to him now, either. It was going to take some getting used to.

"It makes you realise how savage the human race really is, doesn't it?"

"What?"

"The people. The gawkers. They don't make for very pleasant viewing."

Reluctantly he followed her gaze, saddened at the anticipation he saw etched onto more than a few faces. To their credit, some of the onlookers looked sick, some were even offering up a prayer, he thought. But too many of them were getting some weird sort of pleasure out of his fate.

"I wonder why they do it?"

"Do what?"

"You know." He gestured at the crowd below.

"Who knows? I'm sure some of them are genuinely sorry. They're probably praying for your immortal soul right now. Either that, or thanking God that their lives aren't quite that desperate."

"And the others?"

"Some are just plain nosy. They'd get a kick out of anything they shouldn't see or hear. I worry more about the ones that get a thrill out of it. Get off on the blood. It makes you think about what they'd do for kicks when there isn't an accident or a suicide handy."

"That's obscene."

"People are, John, by and large. It's just a matter of degree. Didn't you ever figure that one out?"

She looked away then, began to fade a little. She wasn't quick enough, however, to stop John from seeing the tears beginning to track down her cheek.

"Let her be, John. She'll get over it."

The priest was back; a little more hunched now, a little more defeated. "It took her a long time to learn that lesson. Almost forty years."

"Forty years?" He couldn't believe it. "She looks so young." Harsh laughter stopped him, and he realised how stupid that sounded.

"Of course she looks young! She was only seventeen when she died!"

"That's enough!" Sarah was back, and she was furious. "It's not your place to tell."

He nodded, grinned wearily at John, and faded away. She ignored him for a few moments, then sat beside him, her face averted. She couldn't bring herself to look at him.

"I didn't know what I was doing."

John waited, sensing this was a one-time deal. She would never talk about it again. He could see how hard it was for her. It was written all over her face.

"My parents were pretty strict, liked to keep me on a tight rein, as my father put it. I wanted to be an actress, wanted it more than anything. My father said it was one step above being a prostitute." She swallowed hard, desperately trying to keep control. "He also said that, useless as I was, it wouldn't be long before I took that step down." She stopped then, and John began to think she wasn't going to tell any more. "It turns out he was right."

"You're not like that, Sarah."

"How the hell do you know? We've only just met, John. You don't know me."

There was nothing he could say to that, was there? She was

right.

"I met a man. He was the drama teacher at my school. He said I had talent, that I could go far. Of course, it was exactly what I wanted to hear, wasn't it? I looked up to him, trusted him. When he asked me to go for a drink with him, I thought I'd die. He treated me like a grown up! He treated me as if I mattered!"

"You slept with him."

She couldn't answer, just hung her head, tears streaming down her face.

Sighing, John continued. "Let me guess. He couldn't, or wouldn't, help you become an actress." She shook her head, swallowing hard. "And your father found out?" A nod. "That doesn't make you a prostitute, Sarah."

"I know that." She wiped her eyes, attempted a smile. "But that's not the worst of it." Silence again. John waited, patiently, and finally Sarah looked up once more. "What, you can't guess?"

"Hey, it's your story, Sarah."

"You know. I can see it on your face. I got pregnant. And in the fifties that was just about the worst thing a single girl could do. I hid it for as long as I could, but he spotted it in the end. I was five months pregnant by then."

"What did he do?"

"He did what any self-respecting father of the time would do. He threw me out of the house."

"What, just like that?"

Sarah smiled, a tight, hard little smile that held no humour. "Of course just like that. He didn't want the neighbours to think that he condoned such wanton behaviour. He threw my coat at me, grabbed my arm, and pushed me out of the house. I heard him lock the door behind me."

"Where was your mother?"

"My mother was crying in her bedroom. My father sent her there, and she would never have contradicted him." Now her face was hard, set in bleak lines that aged her in the worst way. "I had nowhere to go except to the father's house. I thought he'd look after me." She smiled cynically. "I was only seventeen. What did I know?"

"I take it he was less than enthusiastic."

"Oh, it was worse than that. He was married. His wife answered the door, and I ran away. I came up here, and, well, you know the rest."

They were silent then for a little while. There didn't seem to be anything else to say. She hadn't just killed herself, had she? She had taken her child's life as well.

*

Time passed. The days blurred into one another, spring passing into summer, into autumn. To John, there seemed to be something missing. There was no sense of being punished, no suffering. There was, in fact, nothing at all.

Maybe that was the point.

He would spend hours, days sometimes, discussing the ills of the world, and where it had all gone wrong with the others. There didn't seem to be any answer that they could see.

Then there came a day that seemed unlike all the others, a day that was so restless it seemed almost to hum. He sensed Sarah when she materialised beside him, and turned to her.

"Sarah, what day is it?"

"New Year's Eve. You know, out with the old, in with the new."

"Something's coming, Sarah. Something big."

"I know. I can feel it, too." She sighed, and stretched languidly. "At least it will make a change."

It was dusk when he heard the car screeching to a halt on the bridge. After a minute the door slammed, and footsteps stumbled towards him.

He heard a baby cry. A woman shushed it, half-crying, and his world came crashing down on him.

"Angie." Sarah drew close. "What do I do, Sarah? How do I stop her?"

"She can see you if you want her to. Remember that."

There was a muffled sob, and then she appeared over the top of the railings. The baby was in a sling, crying. Angie clung to the railings as she inched her way down towards the ledge. A couple of times she slipped, and just managed to save herself. Gradually she managed to disentangle herself from the railings and sit on the ledge

Now, he thought. *Now's the time.*

"Angie." She started, swung around to see who had spoken. When she saw who it was he thought she would pass out.

"John? Is that really you?"

"It's me, love. I'm here." She was taking it surprisingly well, he thought. No hysterics, no screaming.

"You left me, John. You left me all alone."

"You left me first, don't forget that."

She almost rose to the bait, he saw. But she bit her lip, held back the retort that burned to fly. She wouldn't have done that a year ago. Maybe she had grown up a bit, after all. The past year hadn't been kind to her, he saw. There were the beginnings of what would, in time, be some pretty deep lines etching themselves into her face.

"You're right. Okay? You're right. I left you out in the cold, to deal with it all on your own." She smiled bitterly, looked sideways at him once more. "There. Are you happy now?" She wiped a tear that threatened to betray her resolve. "I said it."

And what had it cost her, he wondered? How much effort had it taken her to admit that it had been in any way her fault? She sat there, absentmindedly cradling the baby against the cold, and he saw suddenly what it was she wanted.

Absolution.

She needed to be told that it was all right, it wasn't her fault. And if he couldn't give her that, then it was over.

A year ago, he would have crawled over hot coals to have her back. He would have said whatever she wanted to hear. Now, he wasn't so sure. But he wasn't about to let her kill his son. Life was too short.

Abruptly, the baby began to bawl, demanding her attention. Diverted, Angie crooned softly to the child, hugging it closer.

"Ssshh, John, Ssshh."

"You named him after me." John was surprised, though he supposed he really shouldn't have been.

"Who the hell did you think I'd name him after?"

"I didn't mean it like that, Angie. You know I didn't." She turned away slightly, deflated once more.

"Did it hurt?"

"What?"

"When you… you know." She gestured over the edge, not quite ready to look for herself.

"It hurt like hell, if you must know. Worse than I ever thought anything could hurt. Is that enough detail for you?" He stopped himself, bit back the anger. If he carried on like this, she'd be over the edge in no time. And she'd take his son with her. He sensed Sarah nearby, tense and ready. "It's not what you think, Angie. You don't go to hell, or purgatory, or anything like that. You just get stuck where you die."

"That's it?"

"That's it."

She considered this for a moment; he could almost hear the cogs in her little brain turning. She was obviously finding it all too much too deal with, and the drama of the pining girlfriend leaping to her death to rejoin her lost love would hold a fascination for her. He had to stop that. He had to find something she could hang onto.

"You won't keep the baby, you know."

"What?"

"The baby. He won't be a suicide." She was looking at him, wide-eyed.

"He'll be a murder victim."

She shrank back from him, horrified. She was clutching the baby tight to her chest, and the tired and frightened child began to struggle anew. She was edging back towards the railings, he saw, uncertain now. Then there was a screech of brakes, and a door slamming, and someone running hell for leather towards them.

"Angie! Angie!" It was a man, about thirty, desperate, John saw. He looked as if under other circumstances he would have had a kind face. "Come home, Angie, please. I didn't mean it."

John turned to Angie once more. "What does he mean, Angie?

What's he sorry for?"

"We were having a row." She grinned fiercely. "I can't even remember what it was about. I told him he could get out if he wanted, and he said…" tears were welling once more, and this time she made no attempt to wipe them away. "He said not many men would be prepared to take on someone else's kid." She straightened her back, chin stuck resolutely out. "I didn't stop to listen to any more. I grabbed the baby and came here. I suppose I thought the boy should be with his real dad." She shifted the baby up onto her shoulder. "But I guess it's too late for that, isn't it?"

"I suppose it is." She turned away from him then, made to grab the railings and her life. John was a little distressed at how small the pang that he felt was. Her boyfriend was there, eager to help, and as he reached for the baby both he and Angie were smiling.

*

Afterwards, he couldn't have said exactly how it happened. One minute Angie was passing the baby over the railings, the next the boyfriend had lost his grip and the baby was falling over the edge. Angie was reaching for him, screaming his name even as she toppled over the edge after him. Her lover wailed, and then… John willed himself to Angie and in an instant was there, holding her tight. Amazed, he fought to keep concentration. He had no idea how he was doing this, but he didn't dare let her slip. He concentrated on the ledge and they began to rise. She was still screaming for the baby, and belatedly John realised he hadn't heard it make a sound.

Then Sarah was there. She had his son in her arms, and she was smiling. They'd done it.

They reached the safety of the road and handed their stunned charges over to a boyfriend who looked as if he was about to faint. Then again, John supposed, it wasn't every day you saw such things. Revelations were carefully rationed for a reason. He watched as the boyfriend bundled them into the car and took off at top speed.

Then they were back on the bridge.

"Is that it, Sarah? It's back to… nothing?"

Sarah had the good grace to look a little deflated, but she had no answer for him, just an attempt to lighten the load.

"Hell, at least it broke the routine, right?"

John couldn't answer. He felt as if he were on fire. He realised that for the last year he hadn't physically felt anything. Now he could feel everything. He could feel the heat spreading through him. And there was a light. It felt like he was basking on a warm beach early on a summer morning.

Turning to Sarah, he saw she too was bathed in the light.

Abruptly the priest appeared, just outside the light. He was crying as if his heart would break. He was reaching towards them, towards the light, but something was holding him back.

"A life for a life," John thought. "Is it really that simple?" He doubted it, but he'd learn whatever else there was with Sarah, so that was okay. He wouldn't be alone anymore.

The Last Ghost

"I hate this place."

Lainey opened her eyes with those now-familiar words still on her lips, disturbed by how much effort even that took lately. Her eyes—and lips—were hot, dry, and she wondered if she was running another fever. Or maybe that should be 'still running a fever'. The ceiling above her head was looking a little worse for wear, fine cracks inching across from a patch near the window where a chunk of plaster had fallen away and now lay in bits on the floor. As she watched, the cracks widened slightly, and at almost the same time she felt the room shake. Just a little, the movement so slight she might have imagined it—there was a sense of being jarred, rather than shaken outright. And yet the room was quiet, no one called out in panic or sought to reassure her, as they normally would when something like this happened—no one was surprised by such things anymore; it was almost expected.

"Mum?" There was panic in her voice, so she knew she must be scared—and yet she felt strangely detached from it all; as if it were happening to someone else, and she was merely observing.

"I'm here."

And there she was. Lainey turned her head a little, relieved to see her mother's careworn face looming over her as she leaned forward in the chair next to Lainey's bed. She looked so *tired*.

"You okay?" she asked, watching her daughter carefully.

Lainey nodded, already drifting back to sleep. "Uh huh," she whispered. "Just wanted you, that's all." She noticed the IV in the corner of her vision, drip-drip-dripping something into her arm. "What was that?"

"What, the bang?"

"There was a bang? Didn't notice. No, the shaking. Bomb?"

"No, love," her mother said. "Earthquake. A little one."

Lainey nodded, not really caring that much now things were

calm and she was getting sleepy. And then she was gone, drifting in a warm, dark sea; carried away from all the pain, just for a little while.

*

In her dreams, Lainey loved to run and play. Even though she was fifteen (almost sixteen), and too old really for such things, when she was asleep she went right back to childhood—enjoying games of 'fetch' with Buster, her dog; or Frisbee on the beach with her parents, laughing when they ran out of breath and persuaded her to stop long enough to go for an ice cream, long before there was any chance she'd do the same. As she grew older they'd stayed closer to home as travel grew more dangerous, but these were among some of her most precious memories—times she liked to revisit often.

In her dreams, Lainey was whole. Her skin was bright and clear, untouched by any blemish, her smile bright, white, as the breeze pushed her flaxen hair back off her face and the sun shining in the clear blue sky warmed her skin and coaxed freckles into being. She liked to laugh, when she was asleep. She liked to laugh because, on some level, even when asleep, she knew when she woke she'd have forgotten how.

*

When Lainey surfaced again, the light was fading from her room—a colder, crueller light than that of her dreams. Her breath caught in her throat at the sorrow she felt at being back here, alone in the hospital. Except she wasn't. Her mum was still there, dozing in the chair beside the bed, devoted as always. Lainey watched her, saddened that she looked so old now, deep lines etched in her forehead and her skin pale and dry. She'd lost weight, Lainey saw. A lot of it. Her shirt was hanging loose, her collar bones jutting out; deep hollows that Lainey could probably fit her hand in behind.

As she watched, her mother opened her eyes, focussing immediately on Lainey. When she saw her daughter was awake, the warmth came back into her expression, and her mouth stretched wide into a lazy grin. "Hey," she said, "how are you feeling?"

"Okay," Lainey said. "Thirsty." She didn't bother to mention the sadness she always felt on waking, only to remember the sickness and the pain; she'd done that in the beginning, but quickly learnt that all it did was upset her mother—and she was upset enough.

Her mother stood and poured a glass of water from the jug on the bedside table, leaning forward to ease an arm around her daughter; lifting her so she could drink. It took no effort; even in her own emaciated state she might have been lifting a doll.

Lainey was resigned to this now. At first, she'd felt so stupid, so ashamed that she couldn't even sit up without help, but not now. She sipped, then started to cough as the liquid seemed almost to swell in her throat. Swallowing was something she found difficult these days, although her mother assured her it would pass as she healed. She felt her mother patting her gently on the back, and nodded as she began to get it under control, trying not to think about the amount of things her mother assured her would pass and hadn't. At least not yet.

"Better?" her mother asked, reluctant to stop patting.

Lainey nodded. "Yes, thanks. Can I have some more?"

Her mother lifted the cup to her lips again, and Lainey drank. She took it slower this time, relishing the feeling of the cool liquid as it soothed her parched and swollen tongue and throat. She turned her head a little when she was done, away from the glass, and her mother placed the drink back on the bedside table even as she eased Lainey onto the pillows. "Okay?"

"I'm fine." Lainey tried to sit up, position herself a little better, but the task was beyond her strength, and she quickly gave up. Once again, her mother was there, picking her up without effort, plumping pillows and easing her further up so she was sitting in a semi-upright position. She said nothing while she did this, her movements quick and careful, not making a big deal of Lainey's inability to do much of anything these days.

"Am I really going to get better?" Lainey asked, once her

mother was sitting beside her again, her expression carefully neutral. "I mean, look at me."

She stared down the bed at her body, her wasted legs barely causing a bump under the covers, her body little better. She wasn't much more than skin and bone, and couldn't remember the last time she'd felt well. She only had vague memories of life outside this room now; it all seemed to have faded into one thick cloud of pain and sickness.

"We've talked about this, Lainey," her mother said. "Don't you remember?"

Lainey didn't. She shook her head, tears welling, and waited.

"You have to be strong, honey," her mother whispered. She leaned forward and took one of Lainey's hands, cupping it in her own. She squeezed gently, but didn't speak for a moment. When she did, her voice was husky with unshed tears of her own. "We don't know, really," she said. "We hope so, and the doctors are doing everything they can…" She looked out into the hall as she said this, her expression almost fearful, but there was no one to be seen. "You need time," she said, and stroked what was left of Lainey's once-thick honey-blonde hair back off her face. "Time to heal, and to rest."

"But it's been ages," Lainey said, and now she was crying. "Shouldn't I be getting better by now?"

Her mother shook her head, tried to smile. "It's not something you can set a timetable for, love. We have to try and get you to eat, to sleep… It's the only way."

Lainey sighed, blinked hot tears away. "I want to go home," she whispered.

"So do I, love, trust me. Rest now." There was sorrow in her mother's voice, and Lainey wondered once more what she wasn't saying.

Lainey was tired. She fought against it, but could already feel her eyes growing heavy. "I just woke up!" she muttered, but it was no use. The dark was closing in again, and she had no choice but to let herself fall into it.

*

Lainey was thinking about school; about how much she'd hated it—although she had to admit she'd rather be there now than here, sick, in hospital. She thought back to her favourite class, History. She'd been fascinated by the stories that made up her home country as it was today—the stories of people arriving, making their way from the East coast to the West, finding a spot they could call home and starting to build their homes there. The constant struggle: against the elements, against others who would try and take what was theirs (either from greed or because they'd been there first and resented the intrusion); at times, they'd had to battle the land itself.

When History class moved on to more recent events, Lainey had found it harder to enjoy the lessons. The fact that people were mean, cruel, seemed to be the main point her teacher was trying to get across to them, and it hurt her heart. Or that people were stupid, too stupid to see what was coming, what was right in front of their noses— and when it did finally get through, they got angry. And sometimes downright savage.

At one point, she'd entertained a dream of being a history teacher, just like her own, Mrs Appleton. Mrs Appleton had been her idol— funny, kind, and passionate about her chosen subject. People. History was all about people, she'd say. About the good things they'd done and the mistakes they'd made. "We have to learn from our past," had been her mantra. "We have to learn from it, or we'll repeat it—over and over, until it finally sinks in."

Lainey hadn't been entirely sure what she'd meant by that—her mind kept flashing to old science fiction movies she'd seen on TV— but she knew enough to know it didn't sound good.

Remembering that, something else sparked in Lainey's mind. Since she was small, she'd heard about 9/11. The Twin Towers. When she was little, she'd thought it was something to do with those movies— the one with the blond elf, what was his name, Lego-something? As she grew older the truth had gradually filtered through—just one more example of people's cruelty to those they perceived as different to themselves. And, of course, they took different to mean threat.

She'd grown used to it, in a way. Everyone had. She still got sad every time there was a bombing, or some guy running around with a sword, even when the news of the latest school shooting broke; it seemed at times like there was one of those almost every week.

The world was sick. She remembered how, when she was small and would still cry at such things, her parents would sit her down and tell her such monsters were rare. Most people, they'd tell her, were decent, and kind, just trying to get along in a less-than-ideal world.

Lainey knew better now.

*

Lainey couldn't breathe. She was gasping, her chest heaving, but no air was getting in. She felt herself being lifted into a sitting position. Someone was putting something over her face, something that hissed and made her face underneath it cold. But now she was able to breathe a little again; it wasn't such hard work to get air into her lungs. She started coughing. Her face was wet. Someone—a nurse, it was a nurse—lifted the mask and wiped her lips and chin and, when she took the cloth away, Lainey was scared. The cloth was red. She was bleeding somewhere, but she couldn't remember why she'd been unable to breathe, what was wrong, or even if this had happened before.

Panicked, she looked for her mother, sure she'd be in her usual place, sitting to one side, as near as she could get to her daughter in this place. "Mum?"

"No, love, I'm not your mum. I'm Nurse Sandy, remember?"

Lainey shook her head. "No. I mean… I know. But where is she? She was just here."

A frown crossed the nurse's face and then she smiled, or tried to—it didn't look real, somehow. She eased the mask on so Lainey could breathe a little easier, and pressed her gently back onto the pillows. "It's okay, Lainey. You're okay now, aren't you?" As she spoke she stroked Lainey's head, wiping sweat away with a clean cloth and smoothing her hair back. Her voice was gentle, the words fading into nonsense as Lainey started to calm down. She was falling asleep again, and she couldn't stop it. Her last thought was to wonder where her mother was.

*

Lainey was dreaming again, she knew. Dreams were the only happy place now; here she could run and play, and curl up on the sofa with her parents—her dad reading the paper, her mother flicking through the channels on the TV, her expression stern. She always smiled

*

"Hi, sleepyhead."

Lainey blinked. The room was too bright, and it made her eyes water. She blinked again, and things came into focus. "Mum?"

There she was, her mouth wide in that smile that said *I'm so happy to see you.* Lainey sighed, and started to relax.

"That's me. You're looking better," her mother said.

"I am?"

Lainey turned to stare at her mother, and found her staring back at her with eyes glassy with unshed tears. She knew that face. "What's wrong?"

The smile fell away. "Nothing. Why?"

"Because you've got that grin you get when you're trying to hide something and want me to think everything's okay, but your eyes are wet."

Her mother sighed, dropping the smile. "There's nothing wrong, Lainey. I just…"

"What?"

"Just didn't want to show you how tired I am, that's all. Happy now?"

Lainey considered her mother. She did look tired, that was true. But that wasn't all of it, she was sure. "Why didn't you want me to see you were tired?"

"Because I didn't want you to worry about me. I want you to rest, get your strength back."

"And that's all?"

Her mother sighed. "Yes, Lainey, that's all of it. I'm just tired."

Lainey wasn't convinced, but she knew her mother well enough by now to know she wasn't about to budge, whatever

Lainey said next, so best to shut up and let her be.

"Okay," she said, "if you're sure." Something occurred to her, then, and she turned to her mother once more. "How's Dad?"

Now her mother looked shocked. She hid it quickly, but Lainey was sure. She'd said something unexpected; something her mother didn't know how to answer. "He's… he's the same," she said.

Lainey wracked her brains for some detail that would tell her what that meant, but things were foggy. "He's okay, then?"

"He's hurt, Lainey, remember? The accident?" Her mother's frown was deepening, and she looked almost desperate as she watched Lainey's reaction.

"The accident?" Lainey couldn't remember any accident; she couldn't even remember when she'd last seen her father, or how he'd looked.

"You don't remember." Her mother's tone was almost reproachful, and Lainey felt herself getting upset.

"I'm sorry," she whispered, "I'm trying, I really am, but…"

"No! Lainey, no! You don't have to get upset, sweetheart. It's no surprise you can't remember. You've been so sick!" She took Lainey's hand in hers and held it tight. "Your dad had an accident at work; the building he was in collapsed, and he was hit by falling debris."

"How did the building collapse?"

Lainey's mother didn't answer for a moment, her expression growing guarded, as if she didn't know how to answer.

"Oh," Lainey said. "Of course." She was stupid. It had been a bomb, must have been—though she couldn't remember who might have done it. There were so many now, eager to show their devotion to some cause or other by dying, or better, dying and killing at the same time.

Lainey shivered. "Is he badly hurt?" she asked, her voice so small now that she could barely hear it herself.

Again that pause, before the too-bright answer: "He'll be fine, Lainey; it's just going to take a while."

Again, Lainey had the sense her mother was keeping things from her, but she knew she'd just have to accept that. She nodded, and closed her eyes; not to sleep this time, but to hide her tears if she could.

Her mother said nothing more, and Lainey was happy to lie in bed, pretending to sleep, safe in the fact she knew no more than her mother thought she had to. She was fifteen-and-a-half, almost sixteen, but sometimes Lainey wished she was much smaller, back in the arms of her mother, or being flung into the air by her father as he whirled her around the park.

*

Lainey was four, and it was Christmas. She was sitting at the top of the stairs, staring down through the bannisters as her parents decorated the tree. She couldn't hear what they were saying, but they were laughing and joking, so all was well. Daddy hadn't been home long, just a few days—Mummy had been worried he wouldn't get back in time, but it had all worked out in the end.

Daddy said something, and Mummy drew closer. As Lainey watched, her father put his arms around her mother and they started to kiss, all thoughts of decorating the tree forgotten. Eww, gross, Lainey thought, and scrambled to her feet.

"Lainey? That you?"

They'd heard her. Lainey scurried into her room and climbed into bed, pulling the covers over her head and laying still. She heard them coming up the stairs, and held her breath.

The door creaked open. "Lainey?"

She didn't answer. Her parents came into the room, and she could feel them leaning over her, trying to work out whether she was asleep or just pretending. After a couple of minutes they turned and made their way to the door. On the way out, her dad said, "I hope she's asleep, don't you?" and her mum answered, "I do. Otherwise, no Santa for Lainey, and that would be such a shame."

Then the door closed and they were gone. Lainey sat up in the dark, working on getting her breathing under control. She'd had to hold it for so long! She heard laughter from downstairs and relaxed. They were still up, so Santa couldn't come yet. She laid back down and closed her eyes, willing herself to fall asleep, their words echoing in her head. She was a good girl; he wouldn't miss her out, would he?

He hadn't, of course. Lainey had rushed downstairs at the crack of dawn on Christmas morning, eager to see if Santa had been cross with her. It wasn't her fault she couldn't sleep, was it? She couldn't have been the only one? Sure enough, Mum and Dad were on the sofa, grinning at the sight of their tousle-haired offspring catapulting herself across the living room to the tree—hopping from foot to foot in excitement as she gazed at all the parcels. The rest of the day had quickly become a haze in her memory—unwrapping presents, Christmas dinner (her favourite bit was the cream that came with the pudding), snoozing on her dad's lap after the meal while some film was on. Crinkling paper, smells of turkey and mincemeat and spices, feeling full... that had come to sum up pretty much every Christmas in her memory and she doubted she was alone in that, somehow. It boiled down to family; to feeling loved.

*

The room darkened, and Lainey looked at the door in time to see a shadow cross the frosted glass. So someone *was* around, after all. She felt better knowing that, and snuggled back down under the blankets as she closed her eyes. The nurse would be along soon, she was sure. It must be nearly time for her bedtime medication. She ached, but didn't want any more of the medicine they gave her for that; not yet. She wanted to fall asleep by herself, for once, rather than be given the medicine that didn't so much send her to sleep as switch her off like a light blinking out. That stuff always made her feel groggy and a little sick, and she'd had enough of that to last a lifetime.

Someone coughed, and Lainey forced her eyes open once more. Had she fallen asleep so fast? "Mum?" she whispered.

No answer. It must have been one of the other patients, but they were quiet now. As she drifted off, Lainey found herself wondering how many other patients there were on this ward at the moment. It was so quiet here these days; when she'd first been admitted (she was hazy on exactly when that was, she knew, but there'd been people around), the ward had been a busy place.

She remembered being wheeled along its long central aisle and shunted into a single room off to one side, at the end. She was alone but, if they left the door open, she could still see people bustling about; she still felt part of it all.

It wasn't like that anymore.

She turned over with some difficulty, wincing as the ache in her bones intensified, and lay looking out of the window. The blinds were half-shut, but she could see glimpses of the outside world through the gaps. It was night, but there was a glow coming from somewhere. The moon? She wondered what time of year it was, and shivered. It didn't feel like summer; she remembered how sweaty it had been all summer, even at night. Was it winter already? Something was falling from the sky, so maybe it was— although snow normally looked brighter, at least as far as she could remember. This stuff, so like snow as it fell from the sky, was darker, as if something else was mixed in with the frozen water. She was reminded of burning paper, her dad laying newspaper in the grate to start the fire off, and little plumes of burning ash floating up as it 'took'. She lay and watched it fall, her eyelids growing heavy, and at some point she passed out again as the sky darkened and that greyish snow kept falling, hushing the normal night sounds of the outside.

*

Lainey was building a snowman. She was nine, and this was the first winter they'd had enough snow to build anything in ages; Mum couldn't remember the last time, she said. It was a bit of a wonky snowman, she knew that, but still… it worked. It had coal for eyes, a carrot for a nose, and Mum had given her little pebbles from the plant thing (terrarium? Something like that, she thought) in the living room for its mouth. They were pale purple, and now it looked as if it had been eating a grape slushie. Something hard hit her on the side of the head, and she yelled out in fright, whirling around to see who'd done it, rubbing her throbbing head. The snow ball lay broken on the ground, revealing the pebble at its centre. No wonder it had hurt so much.

Two boys (big boys; they should know better, Dad said) were running away, laughing. Lainey heard the front door slam behind her as her father stormed out, shouting at them to clear off and leave her alone. Then he was bending down, easing her hand away from the side of her head so he could have a look. "It's okay," he said. "You're fine. Just a bit sore, eh?" She'd looked up at him and smiled, lip trembling as she said yes, and he'd picked her up and carried her back indoors, for "hot chocolate, just the thing."

Dad could always make it better.

∗

"Come on, Lainey, wake up now."

"Wha…" Lainey forced her eyes open, blinking against the brightness of the light shining into her eyes. "Doctor McGraw?"

Lainey blinked as the room slowly came into focus, marred by the blob in the centre of her vision from the pen light thing the doctor used. The woman examining her smiled then, and answered, "Of course! Who else would it be?"

Lainey didn't know. When she'd first been admitted, there had been a lot of doctors to-ing and fro-ing, nurses scurrying to fetch and carry, bring her water or a meal, or something to be sick into. She tried to remember the last time she'd seen the nurse, and couldn't quite do it. It hadn't been long ago, she knew that much, but a while, certainly. The assistants had brought her meals when it was time, but they weren't so chatty anymore, and wore masks. And the meals were getting sparser, the food more basic and portions smaller. Maybe someone on the ward was infectious? Or some new superbug was doing the rounds?

"I haven't seen you for a while," Lainey said. "I thought maybe you'd left."

The doctor smiled, but her eyes were grim, her face pale. "You don't get rid of me that easily," she said. "I've been here so long now I'm not sure I could leave, even if I wanted to." There were dark smudges under her eyes, and she wondered if the woman was quite well. It would explain the masks, certainly; someone around here had a contagious bug and was spreading the love around.

Doctor McGraw busied herself with examining Lainey, but wouldn't look her in the eye, and once more Lainey realised something was different now; something everyone seemed to think Lainey needed protection from. Lainey coughed, her throat dry and irritated, and she saw fear leap in the woman's eyes.

"It's just a tickle, Doc, I promise."

Doctor McGraw smiled tightly at her, then continued making notes. Lainey noticed she was being careful not to sit too close.

Lainey let her gaze wander, past Doctor McGraw, out to the open corridor. There wasn't much light out there, and she couldn't hear anything to indicate there were other people around. Her stomach rumbled, and she was reminded it must be nearly dinner time, but she couldn't smell anything—not even the cabbage that pervaded the ward every time it was on the menu. That smell lasted for days.

"Where is everybody?" she asked, but Doctor McGraw just frowned and kept making her notes.

"Doc?"

"Don't worry about anyone else, Lainey. You need to rest."

The good doctor was being evasive, Lainey decided, and she didn't like it.

"All I do is rest," she said, her tone sharper than she'd intended. "Why isn't anyone around to talk to anymore?"

Doctor McGraw sighed. "You're infectious, Lainey. Remember? We had to move you."

Lainey didn't remember, and said so. "And even if I am," she added, "why can't I hear anyone else?"

"It's a long corridor," the doctor muttered. "Sound gets muffled."

"Not that much," Lainey shot back, gratified to see her surprised expression at the answer. She might be sick, but she wasn't stupid. "Come on, Doc, where are they?"

"I told you, Lainey," the doctor replied, a hint of steel creeping into her voice, "don't worry about anyone else." She stood up and headed for the door, coat tails flapping behind her and her heels tap-tapping on the faded linoleum. When she reached the door, she turned and looked back, and now Lainey could see she wasn't angry, or even annoyed; she was desperately sad. Her eyes looked huge in that thin face, and it occurred to Lainey that she hadn't seen anyone recently that her mother would describe as fat, or even 'well padded'.

"Jeez, Doc," Lainey whispered, "go and eat something, will you?"

Doctor McGraw smiled, an expression even sadder than the hangdog one she'd had for the last half hour, and shook her head. "You've got an old head on you, Lainey," she whispered. "God help us."

And then she was gone, leaving a puzzled Lainey to try and figure out what she'd meant by that.

"It's so quiet," she said, to no one in particular, but wasn't surprised when no one answered. She focussed on her room once more, and realised she was alone. She hadn't even heard the doctor leave. Her throat and chest started to tickle and then she was coughing again, her hand coming away bloody when she wiped her mouth. She started to cry and wondered when her mother would return, or even if she'd come back. She was afraid, and was starting to worry that she'd never go home. And no one would tell her anything.

*

Lainey was thirteen now. She was sitting on the sofa in the living room, her knees drawn up to her chest, her mouth an "o" of surprise as she watched the news. Her mother wasn't home from work yet, and Lainey was laid up with a badly sprained knee—after some misgivings, her mother had allowed her to stay home unsupervised, as long as she promised to call if she needed anything. "I'll be fine, Mum," Lainey had said, laughing. "I don't need a babysitter." Her mother had left food and drink within reach, and Lainey had a walking stick to get around with if she needed the bathroom, or wanted something else to eat... and up to now it had been great. Lainey had watched her favourite film while scoffing a packet of her favourite chocolate chip cookies, and then she'd eaten the sandwiches and can of Diet Coke her mother had left for her. Now she was sitting in a nest of crumbs, still thirsty. She wanted milk, she decided. Milk was the best drink to go with cookies—or to wash them down. She sat forward, brushing crumbs off her top and resolving to get the dustbuster out before Mum got home, and reached for her stick.

Then the DVD had ended and the TV had come back on, tuned to the news. A reporter was gesturing frantically as she spoke into a handheld microphone and frowned at the camera. Behind her, Lainey could see an office block, and it looked all-too-familiar. It was where her dad worked, and there wasn't a whole lot of it left. Lainey wasn't really taking much in; all she could see was the devastation of her father's workplace, and only certain words were filtering through: "bomb", "loss of life", "terrorism"… all words that featured far too often on the news these days, according to her parents. She could hear someone screaming, a sort of teakettle whine that was building by the second, and then she saw someone run into shot, chased by police officers who grabbed her and dragged her back. Dragged her mother back, away from the debris and the smoking hole at its centre.

Her mother had come home some hours later, bedraggled and distraught. Dad was in hospital, she said. He'd been badly injured in the blast. Her eyes had been red from crying, and hollow, and her voice seemed to emerge from the depths of a pit somewhere. Lainey wasn't sure how bad her dad was, but she knew he wasn't doing well. Questions weren't invited, and she didn't want to know anyway; she was content to believe he'd be home before long; the doctors could help him.

*

Lainey opened her eyes and stared at the ceiling, content to have remembered the accident, at least. Everything after that—right up to her current sickness—was a void, but she could remember the explosion on the news, and her mother's face as it had loomed into the left of the TV screen. She'd told Lainey he was still alive, still healing, and that would have to be enough—at least for now. She had a vague recollection of seeing news footage of survivors being brought out on stretchers, her dad among them, but she had no memory of being taken to see him—just of her mother's reports on how he was doing. And her face, the strain etched onto it for all to see, throughout the whole ordeal.

*

The world was on fire. Lainey was younger, maybe fourteen, so she knew this was a dream. It was one she dreamed often, and every time she woke up screaming. She was sitting cross-legged on the living room floor, her tatty-eared cuddly rabbit, Elmer, in her lap. This was another sign she was dreaming. At fourteen, Elmer lay unattended at the foot of her bed unless Lainey was sick, or really upset. She was watching a film, one of her childhood favourites: Lilo and Stitch. Stitch was stomping around, destroying everything around him, clearly having fun. The house shook, hard, and the power went out. Then her mother was there, hauling her upright, turning away from the windows and heading for the basement with her daughter in tow. There must have been a storm, because the next second everything turned white, and she could barely see anything. She was hot, and her skin itched. Over her shoulder, she saw a huge cloud. Except, how could it be a cloud when it was moving upwards and came from somewhere on the ground?

Then something slammed into the house and they were falling, falling down the stairs, falling...

*

She couldn't stop coughing. She woke up hacking and gasping for breath, moaning at the pain that ripped through her chest with every try. She was still alone. No one came to make sure she was okay, or bring medicine. She struggled until she was semi-upright, but that did nothing to help her breathing. Looking down, she saw bright splashes of blood on the faded white sheets and started to cry.

"Mum?" Her voice was cracked, barely there at all.

No answer. Something scuttled along the floor outside her room—a cat, or perhaps something smaller? She didn't want to think about that. Not now.

She raised her voice and tried again, her throat protesting at the effort. "Mum? Anyone?"

She lay there, gasping, waiting for help… and no one came. Lainey didn't know how long she'd lain there when her mother finally appeared, but there seemed to be something wrong with her vision now, as well as the cough. Her mum looked misty, as if she was seeing her in a mirror liberally smeared with grease.

"Mum?" Lainey's voice was thin, weak, and she was shocked by the effort it had taken to force that one word past her dry, cracked lips.

Her mother didn't answer. She looked so sad, just watching as her daughter lay helplessly on the bed, fighting for breath, clinging on to what she was starting to think was a forlorn hope that someone (a doctor, a nurse, anyone qualified to help her) would come.

A breeze wafted in through the open window, and Lainey shivered. She turned her head to look at the window, surprised by the draught. It was never open.

And it wasn't now. There was a jagged crack zigzagging down its length, and a chunk of glass about the size of a tennis ball had fallen out entirely. Lainey tried to see if there was glass on the floor, eager to warn her mother if that were the case, but she lacked the strength to lean over far enough, and gave up before she'd done much more than shift a little on the bed.

"Mum?" she whispered. "I need you. Where are you?"

She closed her eyes against the tears that were flowing now, hot and stinging, and let herself drift away on the breeze.

*

She was sitting on a wooden bench, shaded by a cherry tree in full blossom. She smiled in relief as she recognised her garden, as it had been before… before. It was warm, and Lainey could see her kitten, Pom-Pom, gambolling at the far side of the grass, trying and failing to catch a butterfly.

She wasn't on her own anymore. It took her a little while to figure out how she knew that, and while she was thinking she sat quite still, not wanting to give herself away if it wasn't someone friendly. It crossed her mind to wonder why she was so careful, but she chose not to think about that too much—this was a dream, after all, and who said they had to make perfect sense. Whoever it was brushed a strand of Lainey's hair from her face and tucked it behind her ear, and Lainey started to cry. She knew now.

"Mum!"

She launched herself at her mother, happy to find herself wrapped in the safety of her arms for the first time in what felt like forever, to feel her mother's chin resting softly against the top of her head, and to smell her familiar perfume. She was crying again but now she didn't know why. She was happy. She should be smiling. She was...

*

... still crying when she opened her eyes. She was back in hospital, lying on a blood-soaked bed, and her chest felt as if something had torn inside—something vital. She was breathing in short gasps, barely getting any air, and the air felt so cold now that it burned. She shivered, and winced as something in her side gave, sending a sharp pain shooting through her ribs. She wiped the spittle from her cracked lips, and groaned when her hand came away bloody.

"Where are you, Mum?" she whimpered, and turned her head as far as she could to see if anyone was in the room or the corridor outside.

The door to her room was open, as always, but it seemed to be hanging wrong—as if it was slightly loose on its hinges. It was hanging at an angle, and swaying in the breeze. Beyond that, the hall seemed to be empty. Lainey could see open doors a little further down, and an upended trolley just lying in the middle of the corridor... the place was silent. No footsteps, no one (apart from her) coughing or crying, no voices. She was completely alone, as far as she could tell. This was wrong. This wasn't how the hospital looked, wasn't the usual view from her room. It was quiet these days, that was true, but it always looked clean.

There was never anything like a door hanging loose, or a broken window. This wasn't right.

The door creaked, and there was a sense of… of what, exactly? The room was empty, Lainey could see that (although she wished she couldn't), and yet… there was a feeling that someone was near. She remembered that she'd seen her mother, even though she seemed to have been looking through dirty glass at the time, and wondered where she'd gone. Why hadn't she been able to see her properly?

Her thoughts went quite naturally from there to her dad. "He'll be better soon," her mother had said. "Remember the accident?" Lainey barely remembered that—at least not the details of how badly her father had been hurt; a fact she found extremely worrying. She could smell peppermint, which made him seem close when he'd been gone for so long. Lainey thought back to her favourite memories of them both, and closed her eyes, exhausted.

*

"Come on, we'll be late!"

It was Lainey's first day of school, and she was dragging her heels. She didn't want to go. She didn't want to be wearing this scratchy grey jumper, or the thick woollen tights her mother had made her put on so she didn't scuff her knees so easily. "Honestly, Lainey," her mother had said, grinning at her. "You're so clumsy; people will think you've been in an accident! Look at your knees!"

Lainey couldn't help it. She got excited, and then she ran. And—more often than not—she would then fall over. On this particular occasion, a mere week before she was due to go to "big school", as her mother put it, Lainey had fallen over while chasing a kitten, landing hard and skidding on the wet gravel. Her knees had borne the brunt of the impact, and were still covered in thick scabs, with dark blue bruises around them. They didn't look very nice, that was true. Now she could feel them catching on the grey wool, and she hoped the tights didn't pull them off and make her legs bleed all over again.

"Stop scratching, Lainey."

Her father took her hand, and squeezed it gently. When she looked up at him, he winked, and smiled, and she felt better. Daddy wouldn't make her go if it was going to be bad.

That had been the highlight of the day, Lainey remembered. She'd skipped into school, each hand warmly enclosed by a parent's, with a big grin on her face. The first inkling that all might not be well had been when her parents gave her a kiss and waved goodbye, telling her to be a good girl for the teacher. She'd stood there, smile melting off her face as they dwindled into the distance.

That was the first time she'd ever felt alone. School became a daily ordeal, trying to stay out of the way of the rowdier kids, ignoring the jibes and shoves, or worse, when she didn't want to play something rough. She wanted to read or draw—she was different, and they knew it. It only got worse as she grew older, the shoves occasionally becoming punches or slaps, the jibes becoming meaner and more inventive. Time and again, as the years passed, Lainey begged to be allowed to be home-schooled, to be saved from her tormentors—and time again her parents, although sympathetic, told her she had to learn how to mix with other children. She had to learn to be social with her peers.

She never did quite get the hang of it, though over the years she managed to make a few friends that were like her, preferring films and books to sports and bitching. Her parents assumed she'd adjusted, and was happy, but really she was just biding her time, learning how to get by in a world she didn't like or understand.

*

Lainey didn't have long now; she knew this, deep in her heart. She could feel it. Her body was losing what little strength it had had for months now. Her skin was cold and clammy, her breathing so shallow it was barely there. She lay and watched the dust motes dancing in the air above her head, and smiled. So dust was something like seventy percent human skin; so what? It danced around, carefree, and reminded her that, at some point in her life, she'd been the same. Before school, before life had shown her what it looked like under the skin—ugly and hard, and so eager to brush off on her and make her the same.

She would have liked to see her parents once more first, though. She didn't want to die alone; she was scared, and wanted someone to hold her, and tell her it would all be okay, even though she knew it wouldn't. It was a lie she was desperate to believe, if only to quell the panic she could feel bubbling up within her. Her stomach rolled, and she groaned, anticipating another round of dry heaves, because her stomach was so empty there was nothing left to come up. She thought about turning sixteen, not that far away if she'd been healthy—she'd been planning the perfect party in her head for years: music, her favourite food, her friends… she didn't think she'd have to worry about that now. It was never going to happen. Shame, she'd really been looking forward to it—to being almost a grown up, with more privileges, but still enough of a child to be able to fall back on her parents when she needed to.

"Lainey?"

Lainey knew that voice. She turned her head, and smiled. "You're here?"

Her mum was standing in the doorway, arms folded across her chest, tears wetting her cheeks. She tried—and failed—to smile. Her mother nodded. "I've been here all along, watching you. You were just so sick."

Lainey frowned a little, aware that something in that sentence didn't quite gel, but she didn't want to think about that now. She wasn't alone any more. She could be held, and lied to, and given the comfort she so badly needed.

"I'll be okay, won't I?" she asked, and smiled, relieved, when her mother nodded.

"You've always been a good girl, Lainey," her mother whispered. "We're so proud of you."

"We? Is Dad here?" Lainey tried to turn her head, to see him for herself, but she was too weak now.

"He's not far away. We can see him soon."

Lainey was finding it hard to breathe again; she felt as if her chest was filling up with liquid—it was like breathing through soup. Fear rose in her once more, greater this time, and the truth was crowding in at the corners of her mind.

"Mum, I… I can't…"

"Shh, Lainey," her mother whispered, and now she was clearer. Lainey could see tears in her eyes as she stroked her daughter's hair, could smell that perfume—it was as comforting as it had always been. "Just rest. I'm here."

Lainey couldn't answer, couldn't even ask her to fetch a nurse—not that one would come; she couldn't remember the last time she'd seen anyone else. She was choking, her throat filling with fluid faster than she could even try to cough it up. She could feel the papery weight of her mother's hand; it was barely even there, but she felt her fear wash away under that touch. She sighed, or tried to, and felt peace flowing out through her muscles, releasing the tension and even the pain she'd known for so long. "Is it okay?" she whispered.

"What, sweetheart?" Her mother was leaning over her, head close so she could hear her daughter.

Lainey opened her eyes and smiled. "Can I go now?"

Her mother nodded, and Lainey closed her eyes and let go.

*

It was dark. Lainey couldn't see anything, couldn't feel or hear anything. For a moment, panic started to build in her and she opened her mouth to scream. Then she felt arms wrap around her, and smelt perfume, and she knew—just knew—that everything would be okay. She forced her breathing to slow (it didn't hurt now, and that felt marvellous), forced herself to be still, and focus. Then she opened her eyes.

*

"Everyone's back! Look!"

Lainey was standing in her hospital room. *Standing.* All by herself. It took a moment for this to sink in, and she gazed down at her feet in wonderment. Her legs looked lean but well-muscled, strong—her skin even had a light tan. She was standing on the faded linoleum in her bare feet, wriggling her toes in excitement at this unfamiliar sensation.

"Mum, look!"

"I see!" her mother said, and laughed. "How do you feel?"

Lainey thought about that. "I feel… clean. Does that make sense?"

She looked down at herself, at her hands, relishing the smooth look of her skin, the ease with which she could now breathe; the… the normality of how she felt, after all those months in bed.

"It does. Look." Her mother gestured at the bed behind her, and Lainey's smile faded. She didn't want to turn. Not now. She had a feeling she knew what was in that bed, and didn't want to look at it anytime soon.

"Do I have to?" she asked, willing her mother to let her off just this once.

"It's okay, I promise. You'll see."

Slowly, Lainey turned around to face the hospital bed that had been her prison for so long. The sheets were grey, rumpled, and she could still see the blood on them. She realised that what she saw lying in the bed was her—she really could see herself—and gasped.

The Lainey in the bed was a very different girl to the one she remembered. That Lainey had always been ready to laugh, had been pretty (she didn't think this was bigheaded; everyone had always told her how pretty she was, so she was just repeating what they'd said, wasn't she?), and strong. The Lainey she saw now was shrunken, wasted, her skin grey, turning to blue in places, cracked and dry. Dried blood crusted at the edges of her lips, and her hair was all but gone, just dead grey wisps here and there on that bald skull, and her eyes had filmed over—leaving her resembling nothing more than a mummy unwrapped from its bandages. As she watched, that room—the one she knew to be real, to be *solid*—started to fade into darkness, leaving behind an afterimage that Lainey didn't want to look at anymore. She felt better now, and surely that was what mattered, in the end.

She turned back to her mother, and tentatively reached out to touch her hand. Her mother's grip closed around her palm, and

Lainey was instantly transported back to that first day of school. She held on tight, and asked, "You're not going to leave me this time, are you?"

Her mother shook her head, unable to speak through her tears, and led her daughter by the hand, out of her all-too-familiar hospital room.

The corridors were empty, but Lainey heard voices all around. They were laughing, happy; in the distance she was fairly sure she could hear someone singing.

"Where is everyone?"

"This place can close down now," her mother answered. "Everyone's outside, or in their homes—with their friends, their loved ones."

Lainey didn't understand. Didn't want to. "No one's sick?"

"Not anymore. Come on." Her mother led her towards the exit, and Lainey blinked at the brightness outside the main doors.

"It's warm," she exclaimed, "and so sunny!"

"Everything's better now, you'll see," her mother said, laughing, and kept walking.

Lainey saw a small boy, maybe five or six years old, playing fetch with an ageing Labrador—both he and the dog sported huge grins and were delighted with each other's company. Lainey smiled shyly at the boy, and was glad to see him smile and wave back. Maybe she did look okay, after all.

As they walked towards the town centre, Lainey was silent, trying hard to take in all the details of life around her. The town was teeming with people (and animals) everywhere. No one looked sick, or sad, and Lainey saw no sign of the damage that had been inflicted on so many buildings in the months leading up to her illness. She'd watched the news reports with horror, crying at the scenes of devastation shown day after day. Then there'd been... there'd been the fall (she couldn't remember much more than falling, and didn't actually want to, anymore), and then she'd been in hospital, cocooned against such darkness as the nurses and doctors did their best to help her recover from her injuries. Over time, she'd seen less doctors, less nurses... but they were busy, had more than her to deal with.

Now she thought about it, Lainey realised she didn't actually remember what her injuries were; at least, not specifically. There'd been some damage to her ribs, and a broken collarbone—she was fairly sure she could remember that much. But what else?

"Mum?"

"Hmm?"

"Remember the fall?"

Her mother looked at her sharply, her dreamy expression punctured by her daughter's question. "What?"

"When I fell, remember?" Lainey persisted.

Her mother's tone became evasive as she answered, "I'm not sure I…"

Lainey kept pushing, unwilling to let her mother fob her off; she didn't need protecting from the fall. It was in the past, wasn't it? It couldn't hurt her anymore.

"Of course you do," she said, exasperated. "I remember I hurt my ribs, and I broke my collarbone… but I can't remember anything else. Did I hurt my head?"

Her mother looked relieved. "Oh, I see. Yes, love, you did— no wonder you can't remember it. You fractured your skull, and had a little bleed inside—you were asleep for weeks."

"Asleep?"

Her mother had the good grace to look abashed at that coy description, and Lainey grinned at her. "You mean in a coma, right?"

Her mother frowned. "Something like that. I'd rather not…"

Lainey relented; this was clearly making her mother uncomfortable, and she didn't want that—not when she was out of hospital, feeling better, enjoying the sunshine on her face…

"It's okay, Mum. I was just wondering why I can't remember it, that's all." She stared once more at the buildings, intact and undamaged, and at the people wandering the streets as they made for home.

"Well," her mum said nervously, tucking a wisp of hair behind her ear (a sure sign she wasn't being entirely honest), "it's no surprise, love. You took a hell of a knock."

Lainey nodded. "Sometimes I dream about it."

"You do?"

"I remember the flash, the light, and then I'm falling. And then…"

Her mum had stopped walking, and was staring at her now, open-mouthed. "And then what?" she asked.

Lainey shrugged. "And then nothing. I can't remember anything else; just the hospital and being sick."

Her mum tried to smile, but the expression wasn't sitting right—and that scared Lainey more than anything.

"What? What is it?"

Her mother shook her head. "Probably a good thing you don't remember. It'll come in time, I'm sure." She started walking again, and Lainey trudged after her, trying to understand.

Then it came to her. "How did I get sick?"

"What?"

"How did I get sick?" Lainey repeated. "Did I get one of those superbugs or something? Because a few broken bones shouldn't leave you in the state I was in, should it? What was it, MRSA?"

She examined herself for signs of the marks such a bug would surely have left, but there was nothing. Her skin was clear, and she couldn't see the shape of her bones under the flesh anymore. She looked… healthy. She glanced around, and saw that no one seemed to be ill, or in pain, and once again she noticed how idyllic the streets seemed now that there was no damage. The view blurred as she tried to focus more clearly, and she gasped, ignoring her mother's attempts to pull her onward.

She stared at the building across the road. It was a local supermarket; one she'd been in many times with her mother—she knew for a fact that it had burned down a couple of months before the… before everything. And yet, there it stood, brightly painted, the shopkeeper (hadn't he died in the fire?) standing outside, smiling broadly. She forced herself to focus, and looked again, struggling to clear her thoughts. And just for a moment, she *saw*.

The frame of the building was still intact; she could see blackened beams and remnants of the brickwork that marked its boundaries. There was an acrid smell to the air, and smoke drifted around the ruined building, the crater at the heart of it.

"What's going on, Mum?"

"Nothing. Let's go home." Her mother tugged at her hand, trying to draw her away from the devastated shop, but Lainey resisted.

"I remember this," she said. "I know I do. So why couldn't I see it before?"

Her mother was crying now, still tugging uselessly at her hand. "I wanted to get you home," she sobbed. "I wanted to get you somewhere safe, where we could explain properly..."

"We?" Lainey turned to her mother, and gasped as she saw something dark forming behind her. It was like watching someone approaching through thick fog. One minute there was just this huge, looming shadow above and behind her mother, then the shadow took on familiar and much-loved features, and Lainey smiled.

"Dad? I thought you'd..."

He grinned. "Left you? Nah, that'd never happen." He opened his arms, and Lainey threw herself forward, sobbing with relief as his grip encircled her, just as she had as a child needing comfort.

"What's going on, Dad?" Lainey lifted her tearstained face so she could see him, and tried to explain what she was asking. "Mum won't tell me. I was all alone, and then she was there, and I was fine, and we were walking in sunshine, watching people having fun, a kid playing with his dog, and then..." She looked over her shoulder at the store, now bright and cheery once more. "And then it was all gone. It was horrible, and there was smoke, and..."

"I know." Her dad's grip tightened, and he kissed the top of her head. "There's lots to tell you, love. Let's go home, and we can talk, okay?"

Lainey stood still, shaking her head, and her father leaned down and whispered, "Let's not upset your mum any more than we have to, all right? She's had enough of that."

He let her go and started walking, an arm scooped across her shoulders as he half-led her towards home.

*

What felt like mere minutes later, Lainey was standing in front of their house—staring up at the gabled roof and huge windows, remembering the way the cat used to sit on her bedroom window ledge and watch for her to come home. There was no cat now. The house looked as it always had, but there was something that didn't ring true about it. Lainey had to wonder whether that was because she'd been away for so long, or if she wasn't really seeing what was in front of her.

"Relax," her dad said, and walked ahead to open the front door. "It doesn't have to be so complicated." He pushed the door inward and disappeared inside.

She followed cautiously, her mother bringing up the rear, and found herself in the living room a moment later. Finally, she felt as if she was really home. She went straight to her favourite spot, the huge armchair by the window—it had her favourite cushions, and her cuddly rabbit, Elmer. She'd missed this; missed just snuggling into a cosy chair and watching the world go by at a safe distance—it was something she'd loved to do before it all went wrong.

She shivered, and just for a moment the room flickered, images of decay and neglect superimposing themselves over everyone and everything she loved. No, she wouldn't look at that. She was home. Mum and Dad were here. She was safe.

"That's right."

"I'm sorry?" Lainey stared at her mother in shock. She hadn't said that out loud, she was sure.

"You don't have to, love," her mum said. "Haven't you realised that yet?"

Her dad was smiling, watching as a range of emotions flickered across her face in quick succession—fear, shock, irritation… He'd always said watching her thinking was better than the telly. If it was in her head, it was on her face, simple as that.

"You can hear me thinking?" Lainey asked, amazed at this new, unexpected turn.

Her dad nodded. "You hadn't noticed that yet? Never mind—it wouldn't have taken you much longer, now you're home." He sat on the sofa and spread his arms along its back the way he always had, sighing in contentment.

He was speaking, actually speaking, and belatedly Lainey realised that was for her benefit. She turned to look at her mother, who was hovering just inside the living room door, her expression nervous.

Her mother nodded, and smiled encouragingly at her. "It's fine, love. You'll see."

Lainey turned to stare out of the window, where she could apparently see bright sunshine and a clear summer's day. "Show me."

"Are you sure?" her dad asked, followed by a muttered, "Lainey, no," from her mother.

She nodded. "I want to see it. I want to see everything."

The world before her fell away. Lainey was still sitting in her living room, and the house was in one piece—so it seemed they'd escaped the worst of it—but the streets were devoid of life. Everyone out there was dead, their bodies decaying or, worse, just a shadow on a wall, burned onto its surface in the conflagration that had changed everything. Lainey turned to look at her parents, but now they were creatures from a nightmare: burned, scarred, sores leaking on the surface of what little had been left undamaged by the initial blast. Lainey started to cry.

"I didn't fall down the stairs, did I?" she asked, crying harder at the look of sorrow and resignation on her parents' faces. "We were *blown* down them."

"I'm afraid so," her mother whispered, and Lainey was relieved to see that the illusion of health had returned to her features. She had no need to see the truth laid bare again; she knew it now: this… this was a kindness, and she was grateful for it.

"And Dad?"

"Killed at work by a suicide bomber. I was trying to get home to you two. I'd heard the warning that there was some imminent threat to security. I thought I'd be better at home, with my family." He wiped his eyes, coughed, and went on: "I didn't even make it out of the building. The bastard triggered the device in the foyer and the whole thing came down on top of me."

Lainey was horrified. She knew it was true, it fitted the details of her dream perfectly, but still it hit hard. She remembered her mother's face as it had looked in the images on the TV screen, and turned to her again now.

"Mum?"

Her mother sighed, the sound like wind in a cave, a sound greater by far than anything a human should be able to make. "We saw the light, remember? Off in the distance. And then trees started to blow over, their leaves in flames, and the wind was rushing... *racing* towards us. I grabbed you and ran for the basement, and the impact hit as we opened the cellar door. The rest you know, I think."

Lainey found that she did. "So it wasn't just a few broken bones, was it," she said, her voice flat and uninflected. "It was what, radiation sickness?"

Her mother nodded.

"And that would be why the hospital got emptier and emptier?"

Again that nod.

Lainey knew there was something else here, a bigger truth. Her mind was prodding the edges of this truth, but didn't want to push too far. She didn't want to know, she knew that much. But she also knew she had to.

"How many are left?" she asked, and now she was crying all over again. Her bones ached, and her lips were as dry as when she'd been lying in the hospital all that time; she felt that same insane itch deep inside that would never quit, no matter how hard she scratched, even when her skin was raw and bleeding.

Her dad came over and knelt in front of her as she curled up in her chair, his face now deadly serious. He looked as if the world had fallen on him, and he'd never be able to bear the weight of life again. "I think you know," he said.

Of course, she did.

"It was everywhere, wasn't it?" she whispered. "Everywhere."

Her mother moved to her side, leaned against the chair, and stroked Lainey's head. "It was very quick," she whispered. "Minutes, that's all. Once one was in the air, everyone sent theirs up."

"And then?"

"And then it was all over, and the few who were left were

dying slowly, even if they didn't know it." She hugged Lainey fiercely. "We didn't want you to know. Your dad and I, we were gone... all we could do was watch as the rescue services found you in the basement and loaded you into an ambulance, took you to the hospital. They were telling people it was survivable then, you see. Lying to us. As if they ever did anything else. The doctors had their hazmat suits, as did the nurses... The few that survived wanted to believe them, of course, and they had no way of knowing what was going on outside."

"What was going on?" Lainey's voice had grown small and thin, as if she were tiny again. She wanted to cuddle her toy and watch Disney movies with her mum, and be safe. She wanted more than anything to be safe.

"Things were breaking down," her dad carried on. "So few survivors, everything irradiated... even those left walking were already dead, if they but knew it. You were safe inside, and all we could do was wait."

"You saw me sometimes," her mum said, and now it was clear she was trying to cheer Lainey up—her voice had that bright, singsong quality it always had when she was trying to convince her daughter things were all right really. "Remember?"

Lainey nodded. "The nurses didn't mention you much."

Her mother smiled sadly. "They couldn't see me."

"No," Lainey replied, "but they used to tell me you'd be proud of me. I was a good girl, they said, and you'd be proud."

"And I was."

Lainey thought back. "And then the nurses didn't come anymore. No one did. And I was coughing up blood, and crying, and calling for you, but you didn't come."

"I wanted you to see me," her mother said. "I really did. I was there, but you were too sick to notice me."

"Too sick," Lainey whispered, and her eyes widened. "And then you were there, and I was fine." She paused, looked around at the familiar living room, at her mother and father. "I died, didn't I? It's over. I died."

It was. Lainey could see it in their eyes; could feel the truth of it deep inside.

"But…"

"You had to figure it out for yourself, love," her mother said. "We couldn't help you. You could barely see us, let alone hear us."

"So I'm what, a ghost?"

"We all are," her dad replied, and held her mother tight as he ruffled Lainey's hair. "But you… you're special."

"How, Dad?" Lainey asked, tears streaming down her face.

"You're the strongest of us all. Don't you know that?"

"How?" Lainey was bawling now, devastated that everything was gone, everything dead.

"You're the last of us, love," her mother said. "We're so proud you were the last one."

"I was?"

"You lasted longer than anyone," her mother said, nodding, and now Lainey could hear people outside, children laughing, dogs barking. She could hear everyone. "You're the last ghost."

Story Notes

Someone To Watch Over You

When editor Paul Finch asked me to write a story for his anthology *Terror Tales of London*, he suggested I might like to write something about Finchley (as I'd lived there for about fifteen years before moving to Derbyshire). I thought about it, and remembered East Finchley station, which is an Art Deco building, still untouched. It's also the first open air station heading north out of the city on the Northern Line (Barnet branch). I love ghost stories, and the more I thought about the station, the more I saw an old-fashioned character saving women who were about to be attacked. I could almost smell the tobacco smoke. Old Holborn, a brand my dad smoked years ago when he tried a pipe. From there the rest flowed quite easily, and this is a story I really enjoyed writing. The story was then chosen by Johnny Mains to be reprinted in *Best British Horror 2014*.

The Cradle in the Corner

This story was the result of a request for a ghost story from editor Ian Whates, for his anthology *Hauntings*. As happens so often, I started to think about what to do while I was going to sleep; and dreamed of a cradle. A very old cradle, which needed a new baby to go in it, but was still occupied by its previous owner. It was subsequently reprinted in e-book form, again by Ian Whates of NewCon Press, in *Obsidian: A Decade of Horror Stories by Women*.

Play Time

You might have noticed by now that I'm rather fond of ghost stories. I was asked to contribute a story to an anthology called *Darc Karnivale*, with no specific guidelines other than word length and that it should be scary. I started to see a park playground, specifically a roundabout whirling around, alone and neglected. Spinning on its own, in other words. From there I found the character of a little dead girl, Mary. She's fed up of being alone, and blames the world, and adults in particular, for her being in that condition. She likes the playground, and wants to play. She just needs a playmate. And a new mother. The story was reprinted in the *Terror Tales* anthology.

In The Howling of the Wind

I wrote this one for a Festive issue of an ezine, *Estronomicon*. It's no secret that I love ghost stories, and this gave me a chance to set one at Christmas, a classic time for such a tale. I had an idea about a boy trapped in a house, the wind howling outside, the boy just waiting for his parents to come home, begging his grandfather for information about when they're coming back. After that, the story almost seemed to write itself, and even now I'm pretty happy with the result. I read this out one Christmas, at an event in Derby. I made half the audience cry.

Sleeping Black

When editor Steve Shaw of Black Shuck Books asked me to contribute a story to *Great British Horror volume 2, Black Satanic Mills*, it took me a while to come up with something I thought could work. While I was researching British industry I came across horrific stories of how chimney sweeps' masters treated the children entrusted (or condemned) to their care, and "'Sleeping Black' was born.

Suicide Bridge

This one takes me back quite a way. It's the first story I had accepted for publication, even though my second, 'Alsiso', pipped it to the post in making it to print. It was published online three years before it sold to a print magazine and a story of mine was finally on paper. I kept dreaming about a man on a bridge, ready to die because he's alone again and everything seems hopeless, except then he meets a girl and falls in love. Where I grew up, there's a bridge known locally as Suicide Bridge for obvious reasons, so the locale for the story wrote itself, really. The bridge itself is adjoined by a path known to fans of "The Inhuman Condition" by Clive Barker; something I was delighted by when I read *The Books of Blood* on its publication some years before. I love reading fiction set in areas I know well; it adds something to the experience, for me. Every so often I get asked why I wrote a story about suicide, but it's not really about that at all. It's a love story; it's just that the main characters are dead.

The Last Ghost
The idea for this story has been in my head for a while, though it took me quite some time to figure out what was, I hope, the best way to tell it. I had the idea of Lainey, a young girl not-quite-grown, ill in hospital with no idea of what's going on outside, or where her loved ones are, when they're not with her. What's happened, of course, is that the human race ruined everything, as it's almost certain to do at some point, given the right triggers. Lainey's the last one alive, the last one to become a ghost, existing in a better world that humans can't ruin. Because they've already done their worst, and it was terrible.

Handwritten first draft of 'In the Howling of the Wind'.

In The Howling of The Wind

The old man watched as the child pressed close to the window, staring wide-eyed at the snow as it fell – flakes large & small dancing in the moonlight. He shivered as a sudden draught swept into the room – the door swinging inward.

It was nothing. 'Just the wind,' he muttered to himself.

The child turned towards him, his eyes full of questions, and the old man felt his spine turn to ice.

"What is it, Grandpa?"

"Nothing... It's nothing, child. Just the wind."

The child stared at the door, & sighed as it swung shut once more. "Do you think they'll come?"

The old man nodded gruffly, clearing his throat as he gestured at the room – the gifts under the tree, laden with tinsel; the mantel laden with cards & garlands of pine, complete with cones & red velvet bows. "Of course. It's Christmas Eve. Why would they not come?"

The boy said nothing, just stared at his grandfather with an intensity he found unnerving. He leaned forward, and tried again. "They're your parents, Matthew. They'll come."

This time the boy responded. "How can you be sure?"

"They love you. You are..." He hesitated, feeling suddenly unsure. "... their flesh. Their blood." He reached out to the boy, who stayed just out of reach.

"Trust me. They'll be there."

Story notes for The Last Ghost.

The Last Ghost Story

A woman, quite young, is listening to the story of what's happened to the world - now a hollow ruin. As the story progresses, we begin to see that the woman herself is a ghost; the last person on earth to die after a terrible war, and unaware - at least to begin with - that she's passed over. The storyteller is an ancestor, trying to ease her into the afterlife and help her understand. The earth is silent now; it belongs to them.

First five pages of a short script of 'Suicide Bridge'.


```
SUICIDE BRIDGE

                                                        FADE IN:


EXT. SUICIDE BRIDGE. NIGHT

It's winter. There's a howling wind, and a leaden sky. The
camera follows the late night traffic up ARCHWAY ROAD. As we
get nearer Suicide Bridge, the camera zooms up so that we can
see a figure, JOHN SMITH, sitting on the ledge, looking down
at the cars.

                                                        FADE TO:


EXT. LEDGE. CLOSE UP ON JOHN

John shivers, gazing down at the traffic. He wipes his eyes,
obviously upset, then stands with difficulty, bracing himself
for the jump.

                    JOHN
          I can't! God help me, I can't.

Starting to cry, he leans back against one of the parapets.

                    SARAH
               (from behind him)
          It's cold tonight.

John whips round at the intrusion, and nearly falls. SARAH is
leaning against a nearby parapet, a tall girl in an oddly old
fashioned summer dress that is being blown against her by the
wind. She doesn't appear to feel the cold, seeming
comfortable even though she's very pale.

                    JOHN
          What? Where did you come from?

                    SARAH
               (voice strangely muffled,
                as if the wind has taken
                it.)
          The wind's strong tonight.
               (she smiles at him, and
                comes a step closer.)
          What's your name?

                    JOHN
               (incredulous)
          John. John Smith.

                    SARAH
               (laughs, delighted)
          I didn't think there were actually
          people called that.
```

                    JOHN
                 (embarrassed)
          Yeah, well. What can I say? It was
          my parents' idea of irony.

Sarah looks at him, disbelieving, and John has the good grace
to come clean. He can't quite take in what's happening here.

                    JOHN (CONT'D)
                 (his voice is totally
                  devoid of any affection -
                  flat and disinterested)
          Actually, that's not true. They
          just had no imagination. Or sense
          of humour, come to that.

He takes a closer look at Sarah, taking in the incongruity of
their situation.

                    JOHN (CONT'D)
          What did you say your name was?

                    SARAH
          I didn't.
                 (she smiles, taking pity
                  on him)
          Sarah. Sarah Ryan.

Neither of them knowing what to say next, an awkward silence
descends.

                    SARAH (CONT'D)
          What are you doing up here, John?

                    JOHN
                 (angry)
          What does it look like, Sarah?

                                                  CUT TO:

EXT. BRIDGE. CONTINUOUS. CLOSE UP ON SARAH.

SARAH takes no notice of his sarcasm, just moves forward and
sits on the edge of the ledge, dangling her legs over as if
she was sitting at the end of a pier. She ignores him. After
a minute, JOHN moves to join her. Carefully.

                    JOHN
                 (softly)
          Look, I'm sorry. I...

                    SARAH
          Forget it.

They sit for a moment, awkward.

                    SARAH (CONT'D)
          It won't solve anything, you know.

                    JOHN
          What won't?

                    SARAH
          What do you think? I can't think of
          many reasons - other than the
          obvious one - for you to be sitting
          on the ledge of a very high bridge
          on a night like tonight.
                    (she glances at him again)
               It won't make some
               miraculous difference.

                    JOHN
               (taken aback)
          Maybe. Maybe not. At least it'll be
          over.

                    SARAH
               (laughs)
          I wouldn't be so sure.

John leans back, a look of comprehension dawning.

                                        CUT TO:

EXT. BRIDGE. NIGHT.

CLOSE UP ON JOHN

                    JOHN
               (realisation dawning)
          Oh, I get it. Isn't this where you
          start your pitch?

                    SARAH
          Pitch?

                    JOHN
               (cynical)
          You know, to 'save' me, bring me
          back into the fold. Isn't this
          where you ask me if I'd like to go
          somewhere 'friendly' for a nice cup
          of tea and a chat?

He stops, looks around

                    JOHN (CONT'D)
          The only thing I can't figure out
          is how you got out here without me
          noticing...

                    SARAH
          exasperated) Oh, please! Do I look
          like I've been born again?

                    JOHN
          No, no you don't.

His eyes travel over her gaunt figure, her pallor, and he
smiles wryly, shaking his head. He doesn't say it, but what
she looks like is an addict. Sarah watches him, anger
building in her face as she realises what he's thinking. She
virtually spits her next words at him.

                    SARAH
          Don't think you understand me,
          John. Don't try to pigeonhole me. I
          won't fit into your neat little
          preconceptions, I can guarantee
          that. What makes you better than
          me?

                    JOHN
          I never said I was better than you,
          did I?

                    SARAH
          Tell me you weren't thinking it.

                    JOHN
          I wasn't. Honestly. I wasn't. I was
          just thinking...

                    SARAH
          Thinking what, exactly? Thinking
          I'm a junkie? Looking for
          trackmarks?

She raises her arms, holds them out to him, defiant.

                    SARAH (CONT'D)
          Nothing! See?

                    JOHN
          No, nothing like that!

                    SARAH
          Liar!

                    JOHN
          I wasn't!

He pauses, before carrying on, shamefaced.

                    JOHN (CONT'D)
          Well, maybe I was, at the back of
          my mind. But mainly...

                    SARAH
          Mainly what? Wondering if you could
          cop a quick feel before you go?

                    JOHN
          No! Mainly I was...wondering how
          the hell I got here, I suppose...

Sarah relents, and relaxes her stance. She starts to move
closer to John.

                    SARAH
          Trouble in paradise, I take it?

                    JOHN
               (nearly crying)
          Paradise? Hardly. Life isn't
          looking too rosy at the moment,
          Sarah, I have to tell you.

                                        CUT TO:

EXT. BRIDGE. CONTINUOUS.

CLOSE UP ON SARAH

                    SARAH
          Oh, really? Well, from where I'm
          sitting, its a hell of a lot better
          than the alternative.

She's furious. Her face flickers, and she lets the mask slip.
Her face dissolves into a semblance of a skull, with her
features superimposed eerily over the top. He can even see
the cracks radiating from a depression on her skull, where
she must have hit the ground.

                                        CUT TO

EXT. LEDGE. CONTINUOUS

JOHN flinches and cries out, and slips backwards over the
edge. SARAH's beside him in an instant, and grabs his wrist -
holds him dangling over the ledge. She brings her face closer
to his, gazing intently into his eyes.

ON SARAH

                    SARAH
               (hissing)
          You want me to let go, John? Do you
          still think it's such an attractive
          choice?

                                        CUT TO:

WIDE SHOT OF JOHN AND SARAH'S FACES

                    JOHN
               (panicking)
          Please God...

About the Author

Marie O'Regan is a British Fantasy Award-nominated author and editor, based in Derbyshire. Her first two collections were *Mirror Mere* and *In Times of Want*, and she's the author of the novelette *Curse of the Ghost* and the novella *Bury Them Deep*. Her short fiction has appeared in a number of genre magazines and anthologies in the UK, US, Canada, Italy and Germany. She was shortlisted for the British Fantasy Society Award for Best Short Story in 2006 (for 'Can You See Me'), and Best Anthology in 2010 and 2012 (for *Hellbound Hearts* and *The Mammoth Book of Ghost Stories by Women*). Her genre journalism has appeared in magazines like *The Dark Side*, *Rue Morgue* and *Fortean Times*, and her interview book, *Voices in the Dark*, was released in 2011. An essay on 'The Changeling' was published in PS Publishing's *Cinema Macabre*, edited by Mark Morris. She is co-editor of the bestselling *Hellbound Hearts*, *Mammoth Book of Body Horror*, *A Carnivàle of Horror: Dark Tales from the Fairground* and *Exit Wounds*, plus editor of bestselling *The Mammoth Book of Ghost Stories by Women* and *Phantoms*. Marie acted as Chair of the British Fantasy Society for four years (2004-2008), and has organised a number of FantasyCons. She is currently Co-Chair of the UK Chapter of the Horror Writers Association, and Co-Chair of StokerCon UK, due to take place in April 2020.

9 781911 143710